MW01612206

Part 1

2017 - Anna

Chapter 1

Sunday 4 AM

S   "I'm going to kill her," Marie muttered to herself.

Her hand shot across the page the clerk had thrust in front of her to sign.

"Not the first time I've heard that," the clerk said under her breath, causing Marie to glance at her. The clerk took the form back from Marie and took a quick peek at it before saying, "You can wait over there. She'll be out soon."

Marie stormed over to the waiting area, trying to avoid returning the glances of the others already waiting. The cold fluorescent lights glared down at her, casting an unpleasant glow on the bare essential chairs sitting along the wall. Marie sighed and chose the chair at the end of the row, perched herself on the rickety contraption, and pulled out her phone.

Marie flipped through her sister's social media posts from the past few days and almost didn't notice when a guard led her out a locked door. Marie's eyes traveled across her sister, taking in her appearance in an instant. Her blond hair hung limp, her short party dress swayed around her, and she held her high heels in her hand, but somehow, she still looked beautiful.

Marie watched her retrieve the rest of her property from the clerk and signed her name on the form already containing Marie's signature. While she waited, Marie folded her arms across her chest and glared at her sister.

When she couldn't ignore Marie any longer, she walked her direction, her head hanging and shoulders sagging.

She didn't look Marie in the eye. "I'm sorry, Marie."

"Anna, I could kill you," Marie fumed, causing her to sink even further into herself.

When she didn't reply, Marie sighed, "Come on. Let's go home."

Anna slipped her shoes back on her feet and took a handful of unsteady steps toward the door before Marie reached out to steady her.

"Thanks," Anna said.

"It's nice to see they at least let you sober up for a minute before calling me," Marie hissed back at her.

When Anna didn't reply, Marie shook her head and helped her walk to the car and climb into the passenger seat before slamming the door, causing Anna to wince. Marie paused for a moment and rested her head on the top of her car to slow her heart rate before climbing into the driver's seat.

"Where's your car?" she asked.

"Still at the bar," Anna whispered.

"We aren't dealing with that tonight," Marie grumbled. "I just hope they don't tow it while you're gone."

Anna pressed her face against the cold glass of the window and gazed at the streetlights passing outside her window. Marie shot furious glances her way every few seconds growing angrier the longer Anna refused to look her direction.

"I talked to the judge," Marie said. "They are letting you go with a fine."

When Anna didn't reply, Marie sighed, letting her anger boil over.

"What were you thinking, Anna?" she roared. "Why would you think getting into drunken fights with other girls at the bar and then getting thrown out and arrested is a good idea?"

"She started it," Anna mumbled. "I was minding my business, and she..."

Marie rolled her eyes, causing Anna to stop mid-sentence.

"Yes, I understand," she grumbled. "That's why she isn't pressing charges. But, that's kind of what happens when you flirt with someone's boyfriend?"

"I didn't realize he had a girlfriend!" Anna exclaimed, throwing her hands in the air.

"Anna, that's no excuse, and you know it!" Marie argued. "Anything could have happened to you tonight! I could have been identifying your body in the morgue rather than picking you up from jail."

No longer capable of making logical arguments, Anna sank her face into her hands, sobs wracking her shoulders. Marie pulled to the shoulder, threw her car in park, and leaned across the front seat to wrap her arms around her sister.

"Marie, I'm sorry," Anna said, burying her face into Marie's shirt, her tears soaking through and chilling Marie's skin.

"I know, honey," Marie sighed.

Chapter 2

Tuesday 3 PM

Anna frowned and looked from the paper in her hand to the building in front of her.

"This can't be right," she mumbled to herself before deciding to walk inside, anyway.

When no one greeted her, Anna again peered at the paper, trying to clear her confused mind.

"You look lost," a playful voice said, pulling Anna from her thoughts.

Startled, she looked up into a pair of dark eyes that belonged to an attractive police officer.

"Um," she said and held up her paper as she felt her cheeks warm. "I'm supposed to go somewhere to pay this, but I think I'm in the wrong place."

The officer peered at her paper and whistled.

"That's a doozy," he said.

Anna looked at the floor and said, "Yeah, I realize that."

"Hey," the officer said, his voice taking a soft, comforting tone. "We all make mistakes."

Relieved at his kindness, Anna looked back up at him and smiled a little.

"This isn't the best choice I've ever made," she whispered while pointing at the page again. "I've made better."

"I'm sure you have," the officer said, still smiling at her. "By the way, I'm Alex Vega."

"Nice to meet you, Alex," she replied. "I'm Anna Hartman."

"Well, Anna Hartman," Alex grinned. "How about we get that fine paid?"

"I'm afraid I'm hopelessly lost," Anna replied, looking back at her paper, the confused expression returning to her face. "This is the right address, but I didn't realize the police station was in the courthouse."

"You're at the correct building," Alex said. "They are remodeling our station and have us in here for now."

Pointing at her paper, Alex continued. "This is the Court Clerk's office, and it's upstairs. Take a right at the top of the stairs, and their office is the first one on the left."

"Thank you so much," Anna smiled. "You've been a lifesaver."

"You're welcome," Alex smiled. "Try to stay out of trouble."

"Oh, trust me," Anna said, leaning toward him and whispering. "If I don't. You'll have to arrest my sister for murder."

Laughing, Alex watched her bounce up the stairs and shook his head when she disappeared before walking back to his desk.

ANNA FOUND THE COURT Clerk's office right where Alex said it was. After paying her fine, she walked back to her car as quickly as possible. She pulled her sunglasses back off the top of her head, she began digging through her purse for her keys, growing frustrated the longer she looked for them.

Her hand still deep inside her purse, she glanced in the passenger window and groaned when she spotted both her keys and her cellphone lying on the floorboard.

"You've got to be kidding me," she said aloud before trying to open the door.

Panicked, Anna circled her car, trying to open each of her car's doors and even the trunk.

When she couldn't find a way into her car, she placed both her hands on the hot metal, looked at the ground defeated, and whispered, "Damn it."

Her head still bowed, Anna mentally groaned when a familiar voice called, "Are you lost again?"

Tears welled up inside her, but Anna shoved them back down and looked up to meet Alex's eyes.

Not able to keep her voice from sounding tired, she said, "I locked both my keys and my phone in my car."

"Do you have a spare key?"

"At my apartment."

"Anyone home?"

"My sister."

"Want to use my phone to call her?" he asked, pulling it from his pocket.

"I sound like a broken record," Anna said, shaking her head and holding her hand out for the phone, "but you are a lifesaver."

Alex smiled and watched as Anna tried to connect with her sister only to sigh and hand the phone back to him.

"She didn't answer," she said, closing her eyes against the tears.

"Hey," Alex said. "We'll figure it out. No worries."

Anna shook her head. "Oh no. You've done enough for me today. I can figure this out. I'll just walk home and get my spare."

"Don't be silly," Alex replied. "I'm not letting you walk home. Where do you live?"

"The Clarion Park Apartments," Anna hesitated.

"See," Alex replied. "Those are on my way home, anyway. Not even out of my way."

Anna sighed and looked out at the busy street that ran in front of the courthouse and realized what her decision had to be.

"I will owe you lunch after this," Anna said, hanging her head.

Alex laughed, "Like I said. It's on my way home. No big deal."

Anna followed him to his squad car but hesitated before getting inside.

"Should I...?" she asked, pointing at the back seat.

Laughing again, Alex said, "You don't have to ride back there. You can sit up front with me."

Relieved, Anna climbed into the front seat and chuckled to herself.

"What?" Alex asked, looking at her confused.

"I think this is the first time I've been in the front of one of these."

Alex shook his head, laughed, and started the car and drove her home.

When they'd pulled up in front of her apartment, Anna looked at him and whispered, "Thank you. You don't understand how much you've helped me today."

"I'll walk you to the door."

"You don't have to do that!" Anna said, surprised. "I promise you I'm good from here."

"Nope," Alex replied, already getting out of the car. "I'm not leaving you here without seeing if you can get inside or not."

Anna grimaced, walked to the door, and rang her doorbell, relieved when her sister called out from inside the apartment. Marie answered the door in her bathrobe with a towel around her head. The moment she saw Anna, her eyes darkened, and she glared back at her.

"Oh, God. What did you do this time?" she asked, before turning to Alex. "What did she do?"

Alex laughed. "Nothing that I'm aware of."

Anna looked at the ground and felt her cheeks grow warm for the second time that day. "I locked my keys in my car."

"And her phone," Alex added, smiling at her.

"I tried to call," Anna added. "You didn't answer."

"I was in the shower," Marie replied. "I almost couldn't hear the doorbell ring just now."

"Well, it looks like you are all set," Alex said. "I'll let you two get to finding those spares."

"Thank you for bringing her home...officer?" Marie said, fishing for his name.

"Vega," he replied. "Alex Vega. And it was no problem."

Anna smiled at him and began walking inside her apartment before turning back to stop him.

"Hey," she called after him, causing him to stop and spin around. "Do you work tomorrow? I owe you lunch...or something."

"I'll be there," he grinned. "But don't worry about it. It was no trouble. I am on my way home."

"Thank you again, officer," Marie said before pulling her sister inside and whispering to Anna, "He's cute!"

Anna swatted her sister on the arm and pushed the door shut behind her, but not before Alex turned to grin at her.

Chapter 3

T uesday 7 PM
Anna didn't want the company, but Marie had insist-
ed on Anna's best friend, Claire, and Marie's boyfriend, Eddie,
coming over for the evening. Even though her escapades would
make for an uncomfortable conversation, Anna hadn't argued
with her. What she hadn't considered was the mini interven-
tion her sister had in mind for her.

After getting Anna to admit the danger she'd put herself in,
Marie and Claire teamed up to cut Anna off from any alcohol
consumption for the time being. Now, Anna clutched a pillow
to her chest and glared at the glass of wine her sister held in her
hand. Marie was too busy making eyes at Eddie to care.

Anna grumbled to herself and tried to force her attention
back to her best friend.

"So, let me get this straight," Claire said while peering in a
compact mirror and adjusting her lipstick. "You got lost, paid
a huge fine, and somehow locked your keys and your phone in
your car."

"That sums it up," Anna grumbled.

"Oh no, Claire," Marie said with a huge grin. "That doesn't
sum it up. She failed to mention that a POLICE OFFICER

drove her back to the apartment when she couldn't get hold of me!"

"Marie!" Anna said, embarrassed. "We don't have to talk about THAT, do we?"

"Oh, yes," Claire said, peering at her friend over the top of her compact. "We DO have to talk about that. You realize you must tell me how cute he was. Spill."

"He was all right, I guess," Anna mumbled, trying to drop the subject.

"All right?" Marie asked. "He was hot!"

"Hey!" Eddie exclaimed, his eyes cutting through Marie, who kissed him and smiled.

"Well, I say it's time to capitalize," Claire said. "Did you get his number?"

"Absolutely not!" Anna fumed. "I am NOT going this route. I'm bringing him lunch tomorrow to say thanks for helping me, but THAT IS IT!"

"Guess who has his number?" Marie said, teasing Anna by waving her phone at her.

"How do you have his number?" Eddie frowned and pulled the phone out of his girlfriend's hand. "I'm not thrilled with you having the number of a 'hot' police officer in your phone."

"Oh, darling," Marie joked and kissed him again. "Anna used his phone to call mine. I don't have it in there on purpose, silly."

Anna rolled her eyes, and Claire capitalized on everyone's distraction by pouncing on both Anna's and Marie's phones.

"Claire, don't you DARE!" Anna said, lunging at her friend when she realized what she was up to.

"What?" Claire asked, pulling the phones out of her reach. "You said you were bringing him lunch. What's the harm in texting him to ask what he wants to eat?"

"Claire," Anna pleaded. "That's so weird. He'll realize how I got his number!"

"It'll just make you appear proactive," Claire said, poking a few buttons on Anna's phone while peering at Alex's number on Marie's. "Too late now, anyway. Already sent a text."

"Ugh," Anna said, burying her face in the pillow in her arms. She jerked her head back up when her phone dinged with a response.

"Oh, my God," Marie said. "Did he text back? What does it say?"

"I texted him, *'Hi! This is Anna, the girl you helped today. I wanted to bring you lunch tomorrow to say thanks but wasn't sure what to bring.'*" Claire said with a grin.

"What did he say?" Anna whispered, her eyes big and focused on her friend.

"He said, *'Hi, Anna! I see you stole my number from your sister.'* Awe, he put one of those laughing emojis in there," Claire said, laughing. "There's more, *'What if we just skip lunch altogether, and I come pick you up for dinner tonight if you're free?'*"

"He didn't say that," Anna said, ignoring her sister's gasp and Eddie's hysterical laughter. "Give me my phone right now!"

"He sure did," Claire said, laughing and holding the phone out for Anna to see before jerking it back away from her. "I'm telling him you're free."

"CLAIRE, NO!" Anna said, attempting to pull the phone away from her again and only sitting back when Alex responded again.

Claire threw Anna's phone back to her. "He'll pick you up in 30 minutes."

"Claire, I'm going to kill you!" Anna exclaimed before darting to her bedroom to get ready for her impromptu date her heart racing with excitement.

Chapter 4

"Ooh, he is hot," Claire said, peeking out the window and watching Alex walk up the sidewalk.

Anna swatted her away from the window and waited for Alex to ring the doorbell. Anna smoothed her hair, took a deep breath, and peeled opened the door. Alex smiled at her when his eyes met hers.

"Good evening," he said, his eyes moving from Anna to Claire, who was trying to peek around the door at him. Anna sighed and opened the door a little further, causing Claire to bound around her and stick out her hand.

"Hi! I'm Claire. You must be Alex," she said with a giant smile on her face. She leaned closer to Anna and whispered, "And you said he was just all right."

Anna cleared her throat to keep Alex from hearing Claire, glared at her and said, "Claire would be my former best friend."

Alex laughed a little and said, "It's nice to meet you, Claire."

"Anyhoo," Claire said and shoved Anna out the door, causing Alex to back up a step so she didn't run into him. "You kids have fun now! Alex, bring her back whenever you want. I don't care!"

Anna winced as Claire slammed the door behind her and looked up at Alex, embarrassed. "I'm so sorry. Claire's...well, she's Claire."

"It's fine," Alex said, trying to put her at ease. "Are you ready to go eat? There's a great little restaurant a few miles away."

"Sounds great," Anna said with a smile. As she followed him to his car, she tried to keep her eyes from noticing how well his jeans fit and how she could see the outline of his muscles through his shirt. But her eyes had a mind of their own, and Alex caught her checking him out when he turned around to open the car door for her.

While trying to jerk her eyes somewhere appropriate, Anna gave him an awkward smile and got in his car. Thankful she had a few moments to compose herself before he climbed into the driver's seat, Anna took a deep breath and tried to get her heart rate under control.

Alex slid in beside her and put on his seatbelt and turned to her with a playful smile. "All set?"

Anna gave him what she hoped was a casual smile that didn't reveal to him how he was setting off every nerve in her body. "Yep!"

"Wait," Anna said when Alex started backing out. She grimaced at him when he looked at her with a confused expression on his face. "I got in trouble over the weekend for not asking upfront. You don't have a girlfriend who will show up in a little bit, do you?"

Alex paused, thinking over her question before chuckling. "That's how you got that huge fine?"

Still grimacing, Anna nodded, which caused Alex to laugh even harder. "Well, you are in the clear tonight. No girlfriend here."

"Good," she replied, a flirtatious smile floating across her face.

Alex turned his attention from Anna back to the road and drove them to the restaurant. Inside, Anna's eyes roamed across the small pub as she appreciated the coziness, quietness, and the charming décor of the place.

Alex watched her inquisitiveness out of the corner of his eye, smiling as her face seemed to light up while moving across the restaurant. When the hostess returned to seat them, Alex placed his hand on the small of her back, bringing her from her distracted state and pulling her eyes back to him. The quick glance that passed between them was enough to make Anna want him to kiss her right then.

Anna smiled at him before allowing him to guide her through the restaurant to their table. During the short walk, she didn't even bother ignoring the butterflies floating around in her stomach. Somehow, they put their flirting aside long enough to focus on their menu and order, but the moment the waitress disappeared, Anna found her eyes locked on Alex's again.

Alex tried to ensure they did something more than just stare at each other all evening, so he broke the comfortable silence between them.

"So, what do you do when you aren't busy paying fines and locking your keys in your car?" he joked.

"Well, aside from getting rescued by good looking police officers," Anna said with a grin. "I'm in college."

"Ah," he mused. "What are you studying?"

"I haven't decided yet," Anna shrugged. "I'm taking a few programming classes that are going well, but I'm not sure if that's what I want to do or not."

"Well, I'm sure you have plenty of time to figure it out," Alex replied.

"My sister has many ideas about how I should spend my time," she laughed.

Alex grinned. "I'm sure she does. What is it that your sister does?"

"She just finished up with law school and is taking the bar in a couple of months."

"So, you have a sister who is becoming a lawyer, and you are now having dinner with a police officer. How do you plan to stay out of trouble?"

Anna laughed and shook her head. When she couldn't find an answer, Alex laughed. The sound of his laughter was making Anna feel giddy, and she took a drink of her water to calm herself down before continuing the conversation.

"Did you always want to be in law enforcement?" she asked.

"I just fell into it. I had a job shadowing gig in high school and decided it was something that I wanted to do. Now, I'm working up to a S.W.A.T. assignment."

Before the two chatted further, the waitress returned with their food, and they did their best to eat a few bites between their conversation. By the time their plates were empty, and the waitress returned to see if they wanted dessert, Anna and Alex had learned quite a bit about each other.

"So, how about it, Anna?" Alex asked with a smile. "Dessert?"

Anna leaned closer to him and ignored the waitress. "Dessert sounds fabulous."

"This was a good idea," Alex said after ordering dessert for them. He leaned closer to her, his hand almost touching hers on the table.

"I agree," she said, smiling at him. "Who would have guessed a crazy weekend would lead to a date?"

A relieved smile formed on Alex's face. "So, we're counting this as a date, are we?"

Anna reached her hand a little closer to his and brushed his fingertips with hers. "Yeah. I think we are."

"Good," Alex whispered, leaning across the table until his lips were mere inches from hers. "I like dates."

Anna's heart sped up as she stared back into his dark eyes. Only leaving her waiting for a moment, Alex pressed his lips to hers, using his hand on the back of her neck to bring her even closer to him. Anna's eyes fluttered closed, and her mind blocked out everything but his kiss.

Chapter 5

Wednesday 9:30 AM

Her professor's voice and the squeaking of his dry erase marker droned on as Anna tried to listen, but the text message resting on her phone was enough to not make that possible. When she couldn't convince herself to follow the lesson, Anna picked up her phone and smiled as her eyes floated across the words again.

She couldn't remember the last time someone outside her small circle of friends and family took the time to send her a sweet text. Now, Alex's was enough to make her heart flutter in her chest.

"Woke up thinking about you," it read. *"Hope you slept well."*

Anna sighed and glanced back to the board to find the professor had caught wind of her distracted state.

"Ms. Hartman?" he said, glaring at her. "Care to weigh in on the conversation? Do you agree with Mr. Bartlett's stance on the subject?"

Anna's eyes narrowed. "Oh, I'm sure I do not, but what was the subject again."

The professor sighed. "We were discussing the concept of AI in technology and whether it will eliminate jobs."

"And his stance was?" Anna asked, pointing at her classmate with the end of her pencil, who narrowed his eyes at her.

"That AI will eliminate jobs, and people will lose their way of life because of it," he replied.

"Oh, certainly not," Anna said, shaking her head and leaning forward in her chair. "AI will change the way we complete jobs. But it won't eliminate jobs completely. You can examine any major technological advancement era to see that to be inaccurate. People adjust, find new skills, and move onto newer and better things. It won't be easy for everyone to adapt, but that's a part of life."

The professor crossed his arms across his chest. "Mr. Bartlett, do you have a rebuttal?"

Not being able to come up with a comeback, the student glared at Anna and said, "Do you argue with me just for the sake of arguing?"

"Sometimes," Anna smirked before leaning back in her chair and ignoring the class again.

"While prepping for your final next week," the professor thundered, drawing attention back to himself, "I want you to write a one-page report for each argument. Each student needs to submit two pages, one agreeing with Mr. Bartlett's argument and another in agreement with Ms. Hartman's. This will be due in one week. Now get out of here."

Anna bounded toward the door without giving her classmates a second thought and blew past the surprised professor with a quick smile, already pulling her car keys out of her purse. Before she made her escape outside, however, someone called her name.

"Anna, wait up!" the voice said. Anna turned to glare at her classmate.

"What do you want, Bartlett?" she asked, putting her hands on her hips. "I have places to be."

"What's the rush today?" he asked, cocking his head at her. "You don't usually run out of class as if the building's on fire."

Anna rolled her eyes and turned to continue her trek back to her car. "Like I said, I have places to be."

"You were distracted today," he continued, trying to keep up with her as she sped toward her car. "You missed at least three opportunities to argue with me."

Anna looked at him and laughed.

"I guess it just wasn't as important to me today."

"Well, gee, thanks!"

"Just being honest with you," Anna said as she reached her car, opened the driver door, and turned to gaze at him. "Anything else, Bartlett?"

"Well…"

"What?!" Anna said, losing her patience with him.

"I was wondering if you might want to argue with me over coffee sometime…or something," he spewed out.

"Oh, I," Anna hesitated. "I'm seeing someone."

"You are?"

"I am," she replied, surprising even herself. "It's new…but…I like him."

"Well, that's good, I guess," he said before shifting his feet and looking at the ground.

"Bartlett," Anna said with a sigh. "It's fine. You don't have to say a magic exit line. Just go."

"Thanks," he grinned and took off, Anna watching him and shaking her head, only glancing away when her phone buzzed in her hand.

"Can I see you again?" the text from Alex read.

"When?" Anna replied, not bothering to control her excitement when he responded almost instantly.

"I have a free afternoon. How about you?"

"My schedule is open. Can you meet me at my apartment in 10 minutes?"

"I'll be there," Alex replied. *"And I'll bring lunch."*

Anna dove into her car and returned home with just enough time to change and freshen up a bit before watching for Alex through the window. When she saw him walking up the sidewalk, she threw the door open.

"Lunch, as promised," he said, holding up a pair of sacks in his hands. "And dessert."

"Ooh," Anna said, raising her eyebrows. "I'm starting to like our dates."

Alex stepped inside, put the sacks on the kitchen counter, and swept her into his arms. He peered down at Anna and slipped a strand of hair out of her eyes before running a finger along her jawline.

Anna stared back up into his dark eyes, and her breath caught in her throat again as he moved in to kiss her. After a few moments, they pulled away but continued gazing at each other.

"We might need to heat our lunch up later," Anna said when she couldn't pull her eyes away from his.

"I think you're right," Alex replied before sliding his hands down her back, lifting her off her feet and toting her toward her bedroom.

Chapter 6

"We forgot dessert," Alex said, smiling at Anna, who lay sprawled across his lap.

He'd chosen to slide his jeans back on before venturing from her bedroom, but Anna wrapped herself up in her comforter and carried it with her instead of getting dressed. She gazed up at him with a mischievous smile on her face, sat up, and pulled the blanket a little tighter around her.

"Oh, I never forgetdessert," she said. "What did you bring?"

"Well, if you are such an expert on dessert," Alex said, getting up to retrieve the mysterious bag he had left on the counter, "I think you should have to guess. Close your eyes."

Anna let the amused smirk stay on her face but followed his directions. Alex paused, taking a moment to study her. Her blonde hair spilled over her bare shoulders, and he grinned at its messy appearance, knowing it had been perfect before he'd gotten his hands on it.

"All right," he said, moving a fork toward her mouth. "What is it?"

Alex guided the dessert to Anna's lips, and she chewed, smiling when he wiped a crumb from her chin with his thumb.

"Hmmm," Anna said, opening her eyes. "It tastes like cheesecake."

"You're right!" he said, sitting back on the couch beside her.

Anna gave him a triumphant smile. She leaned her back against his chest while he fed her a few more bites of the cheesecake and let her attention drift from him to the television she'd turned on when they moved from the bed to the couch. Alex gazed at her in his arms, rubbing her shoulder with his fingers, enjoying the view as she let her blanket pool around her body loosely.

Noticing her distraction, Alex teased, "Do you always pay this close attention to local crime?"

"What?" Anna asked. "Oh! I've been following this story. It's fascinating."

"Why is a missing woman so fascinating?" he asked, turning to watch the news report with her. "They go missing every day."

"This one's different," Anna said, still distracted. "I have a theory."

"You have a theory?" Alex laughed.

Anna sent him a jovial glance and stole the fork out of his hand to take another bite of the cheesecake.

"Yes, I do. I don't think she's missing."

"Why wouldn't she be missing?" Alex asked, confused.

"Well, for starters," Anna said. "She traded her red Cadillac for a gray Camry days before she went missing."

"So?"

"So, did you realize only six to nine percent of cars are red and that seventy percent of cars are gray, black and white?"

"No, I didn't," Alex said, confused. "How do you, and why does it matter?"

"She's trying to blend in. I think she disappeared on purpose."

"That sounds crazy," Alex whispered with a laugh.

"But I think I know why."

"Oh, you must tell me."

Anna stole another bite of the cheesecake. "Money problems. They are dealing with money problems. I'm guessing she didn't tell the husband about it though. He seems upset over the whole ordeal."

Anna turned back to the television. The husband made yet another statement outside the family home. Alex stayed silent and watched with her, mulling over Anna's theory. He was somewhat amused and somewhat impressed with her ideas.

After the husband went back inside the home, Alex turned to Anna and said, "You think they have money problems?"

"Oh, I'm positive they have money problems," Anna said, still distracted by the television.

"How do you KNOW that?"

"Research."

"Research?"

"I've looked into it. Besides, they have a huge house that's worth at least half a million dollars. She's a stay at home mom, and he's a low-level accountant. No way they can afford all that."

"Anna," Alex said, his voice taking a serious tone. "How do you know all this?"

"Ah, a little internet search," Anna said, dismissing him. "They've left her social media accounts active, and I've just paid attention to the news. I bet she turns up in less than a week. Probably hiding out and waiting for the whole thing to blow over before she makes her move."

"Makes her move?"

"I'm sure she's trying to make it across the border or something," Anna said. "She's on the run and hoping she can hide out until the news dies a bit."

Alex frowned at her. "Hmm. Wait! How did you find out she traded her car right before she disappeared?"

Anna cleared her throat and looked away from him.

"Anna," he said.

"I told you my programming classes were going well," Anna said with a grimace.

"Anna!"

"Wait," Anna started with a worried expression on her face. "Am I talking to Alex right now or his alter-ego, Cop Alex?"

Alex shook his head but laughed at the situation. "Lord, you are going to get me in trouble."

Anna turned toward him and gave him her full attention. "I can try if you want."

Alex returned her smile, snatched the fork out of her hand and tossed the remnants of their dessert on the coffee table. He slid his hands under her blanket and smiled as Anna started giggling in surprise. Alex wrapped his arms around her, kissed her, and laid her back on the couch.

"Oh, I'll show you trouble," he said before kissing her chin and placing a few more on her neck, enjoying the sound of her laugh.

Chapter 7

Friday 8:00 AM

Alex sighed and looked through the small notebook he carried in his pocket before glancing back at his computer screen and the new report he needed to fill out. He typed a few keys on the keyboard and tried to immerse himself in the details surrounding the situation. But the abundant amount of noise floating through the office made it hard to concentrate.

Annoyed, Alex's eyes traveled around the small space looking for the source of the excitement. He soon found himself staring at one of his coworkers in shock as he led a woman through the precinct in handcuffs. Unable to react, Alex watched the officer and woman march past him and into a waiting interview room.

When the officer emerged, Alex approached him and asked, "Isn't that the missing woman from two counties over? The one that's been all over the news?"

"Yep," the officer boasted. "Found her hiding out in a hotel. She ran out of cash, and the hotel manager called us over to throw her out. Imagine our surprise when we found HER!"

"You don't say," Alex said, staring off into the distance. "My girlfriend was just saying how she figured the woman was on the run. Isn't that crazy?"

"Girlfriend?" the officer asked. "Alex, man, I didn't realize you had a girlfriend!"

"What?" Alex said his attention being drawn back to his co-worker. "Girlfriend?"

"You said, your girlfriend."

"I did?"

"Uh, yeah," the officer said, laughing. "Don't you know if you have a girlfriend or not?"

"We haven't officially defined it or anything..."

"I think you just did," the officer said, laughing as he walked away to process his suspect.

"Maybe I did," Alex said to himself with a smile before scooping up his phone and shooting off a text to Anna.

"Hey," he typed. *"Are you busy tomorrow?"*

Anna texted back but said, *"I'm so sorry! I have something I'm doing with my sister tomorrow. Raincheck?"*

"Definitely," Alex returned with a smile. *"I'll call you."*

Alex sat back at his desk and smiled to himself and mulled over the possibility of having a girlfriend.

Chapter 8

Saturday 3 PM

Alex looked at the flower bouquet in his hand and frowned. When he'd picked them up earlier intending to leave them on Anna's doorstep, the thought of them wilting before she saw them hadn't crossed his mind. But, since he was already in her parking lot, he decided he might as well leave them and hope they still looked beautiful for her.

He smiled and walked up her sidewalk and cocked his head in confusion when he saw Anna's sister, locking the front door on her way out. When she saw him approach, she turned and looked confused and surprised. He frowned as her expression faded to a mixture of anger and concern.

"Oh," Alex hesitated. "It's Marie, right?"

"Yes," she replied. "I thought Anna was with you."

"Uh, she told me she had something to do with you today."

"Ugh," Marie said, rolling her eyes and jerking her phone out of her purse. "I should have known better."

Alex watched her dial Anna's number and frowned when Anna didn't answer.

"So, she's not with you, and she's not with me," he mused. "Where is she?"

"Your guess is as good as mine," Marie said, throwing her hands in the air before rubbing them across her face in frustration.

"She isn't blowing me off, is she?"

"Oh, no," she said. "She likes you. She wouldn't do that."

"How can you tell she likes me?" Alex laughed.

"God, I can't believe I'm saying this about my own sister," Marie mumbled. "Because she's seen you more than once."

"She normally doesn't see guys more than once?" Alex asked, growing even more confused as the seconds ticked by.

"Well, she doesn't usually see anyone," Marie replied. "Occasionally, she might bring a guy home, but usually, she just doesn't date."

"But she's dating me?"

"She's dating you," Marie said, nodding her head. "So, she likes you."

Alex mulled over the conversation while Marie again tried to call her sister. When Anna didn't answer a second time, Alex began to grow concerned himself.

"I'm so sorry," Marie said, noticing his concern. "You shouldn't have to deal with this. You just met us."

"Deal with what?"

Marie shook her head, "Anna didn't tell you, so she wasn't ready for you to know. I don't..."

"I'm not asking Anna," Alex cut her off. "I'm asking you. You're concerned about Anna's safety, and I want to hear why."

Marie sighed and sat in the chair next to her front door.

"Our mother died when we were little," Marie said. "Anna was five, and I was seven. She had taken Anna shopping, and carjackers decided they wanted mom's car. Anna was already inside the car, so she wouldn't let them have it. They stabbed mom to death as she was pulling Anna out the window."

"Wow," Alex said, not sure what to say.

"Today's the anniversary."

"I'm sorry," he replied. "That's a tough thing for either of you to deal with."

Marie nodded. "Anna's the strongest person in my life. But she doesn't deal with this well. She never has."

"What does she typically do?"

"Get into trouble," Marie said, shaking her head. "She struggles a lot this time of year. I've already had to pull her out of jail once this week."

"So, how do you find her?" Alex asked, but before Marie could answer, both she and Alex heard a motorcycle approaching. Marie jumped to her feet and jogged to the parking lot, Alex following along, intrigued. Marie stopped dead in her tracks and glanced back at Alex with an expression of relief on her face.

"She has a bike?" Alex whispered.

"She takes it because it's cheaper to get out of impound," Marie whispered, rolling her eyes.

"How did she figure that out?" Alex asked, raising an eyebrow.

"Lots of trial and error."

Alex smirked and turned his attention back to Anna.

"Where have you been?" Marie asked as Anna pulled her helmet off and shook out her hair.

Anna ignored her and let her eyes gravitate to Alex and the flowers he still held in his hand.

"Well, hello," she said, her face lighting up as she smiled at him. "Are those for me?"

Alex looked at the flowers in his hand as if suddenly remembering them. "Uh, I had planned to leave them on your doorstep. Since you said you were busy and all."

"Oh," Anna said, looking at her sister and then back at Alex. "Yeah, I might have misled you on that. I'm sorry."

"Anna, could I talk to you for a minute?" Marie interrupted.

"I'm so sorry," Anna whispered to Alex as she followed her sister back up the sidewalk to their apartment. "Can you please wait five minutes so I can explain?"

"I can wait," he said before watching them go inside and close the door behind them.

Inside, Marie swung around to face her sister, her anger spilling over, "Anna, I can't believe you LIED to me!"

"I'm sorry," Anna said, hanging her head. "I just...needed a minute to myself."

"A minute?" Marie asked, looking at the clock on the wall.

Anna looked at the floor, a sad expression passing across her face. Marie's sighed as her anger dissolved. "I guess at least you didn't get into trouble again."

"It's funny," Anna murmured after a few moments of silence. "I went to mom's grave this morning and started to go through my usual routine, but something stopped me this year."

Marie stayed silent, waiting for her sister to continue.

"I realized that if I keep self-destructing, I might miss out on something great."

Marie thought over what her sister was saying before she replied. "You mean Alex, don't you?"

"I do. I like him, Marie. I don't know what it is, but I like him."

Marie let a soft smile form on her face and said, "He seems to like you, too."

"You think?" Anna asked and glanced at the door before sighing.

"I told him what's going on," Marie said. "I'm sorry. He was insistent when he could tell I was worried."

"He shouldn't have to deal with someone like me," Anna said, hanging her head.

"Anna," Marie said. "There's nothing wrong with you. You deserve to have people who care for you. I wish you could see that."

"I lied to him, though," Anna said, not convinced. "I'm sure he's long gone by now."

"I bet he's not. Why don't we go check."

The sisters opened the front door, and Anna couldn't hide her relief when she saw Alex sitting beside it, peering into the flowers he'd brought.

"You want to come inside?" she asked him.

"Hey," Marie said. "I'm visiting mom's grave this morning. I haven't been by today yet. Will you be all right for a bit?"

"Yeah," Anna said, smiling at her sister as Alex stepped inside their apartment. "Thanks for not killing me, Marie."

"Maybe next time," her sister said before wrapping Anna in a tight hug and heading to the parking lot.

She closed the door behind her but hesitated before addressing Alex.

"Alex, I'm sorry I wasn't honest with you," Anna said, not looking him in the eye.

He laid the flowers on the counter before taking her in his arms. "Hey, look at me."

Anna took a deep breath and wiped a tear off her cheek before peering up into his eyes.

He frowned at the tears and said, "I wish you had been honest with me. But we also just met. I can understand why you might not have been ready to share that with me yet."

"Still," Anna said, a few more tears escaping her eyes. "You shouldn't have to deal with this."

"Deal with what?" Alex asked. "A girl who's been through something traumatic but still seems to have everything put together?"

"I don't know how 'put together,' I am."

"Everyone makes mistakes from time to time."

Anna sighed, wanting to believe him. She couldn't help but let the uncertainty floating through her go when Alex smiled at her and put his palms on her cheeks, forcing her to look at him. Alex ignored the wetness from the tears slipping across her cheeks, brought his lips to hers, and enveloped them in a loving kiss. Anna wrapped her arms around him, squeezed her eyes shut, letting him take her away from the pain.

When he pulled away, Alex looked at her and said, "I referred to you as my girlfriend yesterday."

"You did?" Anna said, laughing a little.

"I did. I didn't realize I did it either. It was just natural."

"Natural, huh," she whispered, a lump forming in her throat. "I like the sound of it."

"Do you? I'm glad. So, what do you say? You want to try out the title?"

"Well, I guess if you have nothing better to do with your time," Anna said before standing on her tiptoes to give him a kiss. "I'd like that."

"Then it's settled. Hey, have you eaten? Do you want to get something to eat?"

"I'm starved! I haven't eaten anything all day."

"Well, we can't have that! There's this little café nearby that's good."

Anna grinned. "And I hear they have a great dessert menu!"

Laughing, Alex followed Anna out of the apartment door and waited for her to lock it.

Before they headed to the car, she turned to him, excited, and said, "Hey! Did you watch the news? I was right about the missing lady! They found her yesterday. It was on the news last night!"

Alex shook his head in disbelief, "I was there when they brought her in. I was shocked!"

"You were?" Anna exclaimed. "Man, I would have paid to see that!"

Alex laughed as Anna continued, "They say she was embezzling money from her church and the PTA!"

"I still can't believe you figured it out before we did! You could make a career off that gut instinct of yours."

Anna grinned and grabbed his hand, interlacing his fingers with hers as they walked to his car. "Maybe I will."

Part 2

2018 - Joe

Chapter 1

"I think this is the worst idea you've had yet, Joe," Merida said, looking over the edge of the cliff inches from her white sneakers.

Joe peeked at her out of the corner of his eye and grinned before letting the bungee jump instructor tighten the harness around him. Merida glanced over the edge one more time and tugged on her own straps.

"How do I let you talk me into these things?"

Joe swept her into his arms and tried to kiss her. "You could always just wait up here."

"Why?" she asked, denying his kiss and glaring at him. "So I can listen to you tease me about chickening out on you for the rest of our lives?"

Joe smiled. "I like the sound of that."

She laughed. "What? Teasing me?"

"No. The rest of our lives."

Merida smiled before giving in to his kiss.

MONDAY 6 PM

39

Joe's eyes snapped open just in time to catch himself from falling out of his desk chair.

"Damn it," he grumbled and rubbed his hands across his face.

Those few moments just after waking when his mind refused to accept or remember the truth were the worst. Frustrated, he dug a whiskey bottle out of the bottom drawer of his desk and took a long drink. The glass was cold and comforting against his lips.

Joe tried to talk his brain into functioning and squinted at the lines of code on his computer monitor. But between the alcohol and lack of sleep, any functional thought process was busy swimming away from his grasp.

"It's not working," he sighed, almost allowing the sadness to overtake him.

Growling, Joe shoved the sorrow from his heart and reached for the embedded anger instead, sweeping his keyboard and mouse off the desk, wincing when they clattered in protest as they hit the floor.

He jerked the whiskey bottle back off the desk and shakily brought it to his lips, savoring the burn as the liquid slid down his throat. Noticing footsteps coming down the hall, he shoved the lid back in place and stuffed the bottle back in his desk drawer moments before a knock rattled his bedroom door.

"Come in," he said, grimacing as he noticed the slur in his own voice.

The door opened, and his brother Bryant stepped inside.

"Joe?" he asked. "There was a noise. Are you all right?"

"Yep," Joe replied, trying to keep the conversation to a minimum.

"Mom's made dinner if you want some," Bryant said, frowning when Joe didn't respond.

Bryant looked his brother up and down and examined his eyes before scowling and shoving the door open. He stomped around Joe's room, scooped up dirty laundry, looked under his bed, and peered behind books in the tall bookcase before turning to face his brother again.

"Where is it, Joe?"

"Where's what?" Joe asked, feigning ignorance even though he realized what Bryant was searching for.

Bryant folded his arms across his chest and glared at his brother. Joe attempted to keep eye contact with him but found it hard to focus with the room swaying, so he slid open the bottom drawer to his desk, revealing the almost empty bottle of whiskey.

"I've finished with it for the day anyway," he slurred.

"Joe," Bryant said, examining the bottle. "This has to stop. When will it stop?"

"I don't know," Joe said, hanging his head.

"When's the last time you slept?" Bryant asked, looking around his brother's messy room, his eyes resting on the pile of junk food wrappers piling up on the floor. "Or eaten real food?"

Joe buried his head in his hands, unable to meet his brother's eyes.

Bryant wrinkled his nose and continued when Joe didn't answer, "Or showered?"

Joe raised his eyes to glare at his brother and scooped his keyboard and mouse off his bedroom floor and returned them to his desk. Still refusing to talk to Bryant, he went back to typing while trying to ignore his brother's concerned gaze.

After watching him work for a few minutes, Bryant whispered, "What are you trying to do?"

"I'm building a program to triangulate cellphone signals."

"What's your goal with that?"

Joe swung his chair around, almost knocking himself out of it before addressing his brother. "My goal is to make sure I can find whoever the hell I want, whenever the hell I want to find them."

His hands shaking, Joe swung his chair back around and faced his computer. Bryant sighed and listened to the maddened typing, not sure what he could do to remedy the situation.

"It won't bring her back."

Joe's shoulders sag and his typing slow. "I have to do this."

Bryant sighed and put his hand on his brother's shoulder for a moment before walking back to the door.

"Just remember," he said before beginning to pull the door closed as he exited the room. "I'm here for you."

As the door clicked closed behind him, Joe let his arms slide to his sides, his eyes glazing over. No longer able to keep his tears at bay, a few slid down his cheeks, the growing stubble on his chin hindering their journey.

Chapter 2

B ryant sighed and looked at his brother's closed door before heading back to the kitchen. He ignored the concerned glances his mother kept sending him, made a plate of food and picked at it. His father appeared to be taking the same approach to the situation.

No longer able to stand the silence, his mother sat down her fork and asked, "Is he coming, Bryant?"

"No, mom," Bryant said, not meeting her eyes. "I don't think he is."

"We need to do something?"

"I know, mom. I talked to him already. But what can we do?"

"...Something. He can't keep living like this."

Bryant sighed and looked at his mother and said, "I'll talk to him again in the morning."

"Beth, you need to eat," Bryant's father said. "We don't need you getting yourself sick. You won't do anybody any good that way."

"I realize that, Maverick," she replied. "But I am just so worried."

Silence filled the room again as they picked at their plates before eventually giving up the fight and clearing the table. Bryant made his brother a plate and put it in the fridge while praying Joe would wonder from his room later to find it.

"Let's go to bed, Beth," Bryant's father said when she stared down the hallway a little too long. "We'll try again tomorrow."

Beth gave Bryant a sad glance and followed her husband to their bedroom. Bryant walked down the hall and stopped at his brother's door again, listening to the sound of Joe's furious typing. Before walking to his room for the night, he placed his hand on the door wishing there was a way to take away Joe's pain.

"MERIDA," JOE SAID, grinning and trying to peek underneath the blindfold she had placed over his eyes. "What are you doing?"

"No, peeking!" Merida scolded. "Be patient!"

"Where are you?" Joe asked her, spinning in a circle.

She grabbed his arms to keep him from moving around and laughed. "Just stay still. You will hurt yourself."

"Well, I wouldn't if you'd just let me take this thing off and see what you are up to!"

"Hang on a second," she laughed. Joe listened to her move a few things around and sighed in relief when she said, "All right. You can take it off now."

He pulled the blindfold off and blinked a few times while waiting for his eyes to refocus. Merida waited with a grin on her face.

"What did you do?" Joe asked, peering at the spread of food laid out in front of him. "Did you make all this?"

"Happy birthday," she whispered and gave him a soft kiss.

"You have all my favorites here!"

"Well, not your favorite dessert. I tried my hand at bread pudding."

Joe pulled her into his arms. "I'm sure it's all amazing. Thank you."

"You're welcome," she replied, staring up into his eyes.

"I love you," he smiled before kissing her.

"We better eat before it gets cold," she said, trying to pull away from him.

"Oh, it will get cold," he laughed, pulling her back to him. "Because I want you first."

"Joe!" Merida said, her giggles music to his ears. "Stop it! We are eating dinner first! JOE!"

Joe laughed and pulled her close, capturing her lips with his and putting an end to her protests, knowing he'd already broken her reserve.

MONDAY 10 PM

Growling, Joe jerked himself awake again and rubbed his face.

"Step one," he said to himself. "Shower."

Delirious, he stumbled into the bathroom and turned on the water before trying to undress and find a clean towel.

"Step two," he sighed, staring at the mess he was making. "Drink enough to pass out so I can block out all these flashbacks for five damn minutes."

Joe stepped into the shower and turned the temperature low enough where the water hit his skin like needles. The pain was comforting, so he didn't bother to adjust it. He sighed and watched the soap and water roll down the drain, hoping they would somehow take his sadness with them.

After showering and dressing, Joe glanced around his room, embarrassed. He tried to clean up but the alcohol in his system hindered things. When he gave up, he sat on his bed and picked up the picture on his nightstand.

"I know, Merida," he said. "I'm sorry. I am trying. I promise."

Joe sighed and sat the picture back in its spot and glared at his computer. He glanced again at Merida's picture, scowled and scooped up a pair of earbuds before placing them in his ears. With newfound determination, Joe sauntered back to his desk and read through the lines of code on his screen.

Music blaring in his ear, his fingers traveled across the keys at lightning speed, adding and deleting lines of code as he went. Determined not to let his mind wander, Joe maintained his maddening speed well into the night, stopping only once or twice to wander around his room lost in thought.

Eventually, the typing stopped, and his mind slowed long enough for him to examine his progress. He focused on the lines of code, read through the markings, and blinked a few times, trying to get his mind to accept what he was seeing. Joe took a deep breath and pressed the run button on his program and watched it whir into action. Speechless, his eyes scanned the results.

"No way," he muttered to himself before turning back towards Merida's picture and smiling. "I did it, Merida. I did it!"

Exhausted, he didn't even bother shutting down his laptop for the night and opted instead to climb into bed without changing. For the first time in weeks, his eyes closed when his head hit the pillow, and he spent the night sleeping without the heartbreaking flashbacks he'd become accustomed to.

Chapter 3

T uesday 10 AM
Bryant knocked on his brother's bedroom door and waited for him to answer before turning the knob and pushing the door inward. He cringed at what he thought he'd find, but when he took a step inside the room, he looked around surprised.

"You cleaned," he said, not able to hide his shock.

Joe smiled at him, and Bryant looked back at him, relieved to see his eyes weren't glassed over for the first time in months.

"Yep," Joe replied, crossing his arms across his chest. "And showered. And ate dinner. Thanks for saving me a plate."

Not sure how to respond, Bryant stared back at his brother and shook his head.

When he didn't speak, Joe continued without him, "Hey, aren't you supposed to be at work today?"

Joe looked at the clock on his wall. "It's 10. You shouldn't be home right now."

"I, um," Bryant started while rubbing his head. "I took the morning off so I could talk to you."

"Oh yeah?" Joe asked. "About what?"

"Well, I was going to see if I could convince you to talk to someone..."

"Ah," Joe said. "Actually, I set an appointment with someone for tomorrow."

"Really?"

"Yeah. I figured it's about time to get my act together. Merida would have wanted me to, anyway."

"You have no idea how relieved I am to hear that," Bryant sighed. "Mom will be happy too. She's been worried sick."

"Sorry to cause so much fuss."

"We just want to see you happy again, Joe."

Joe lowered his head. "I'm not sure if I can do happy. Not right now. But I can at least not be miserable, I guess."

"Just remember that all of us are here for you. Whatever you need."

"Thanks," Joe said with a smile. "Now go to work. I have a computer program to clean up."

Chapter 4

Wednesday 11 AM

"I'm here to listen, Joe. But I can't do that if you won't talk."

Joe stared at the ceiling, his feet hanging off the end of the couch, his arms thrown above his head. In the movies, when people seek help from a therapist, this is what they do. He wasn't sure how it could help things, but it did at least give him a reason not to stare at the therapist.

"Are you ready to talk, Joe?"

"Not really," Joe replied.

"The couch is safe," he'd decided the moment he walked in. He couldn't admit to himself that it also allowed him to focus on something other than the situation, his feelings, or the reason he was there.

"Just lay here and stare at that bland ceiling," he told himself. *"It will all be over soon, and then you can tell Bryant you tried."*

Silence filled the air as the psychologist waited for him. Joe sighed and let his eyes drift toward the doctor while attempting to not turn his head to address him.

"I guess it is why I'm here, isn't it?"

"You promised you'd try," he reminded himself. *"Merida would want you to try."*

"You tell me?" the man said, tapping his pencil on the clipboard in his hand.

"Fine," Joe sighed. "Fine."

HE GLANCED AT THE BANK across the street, took a deep breath, and jerked open the door in front of him, cringing at the cheerful chiming sound as the door swung open. Joe looked around and stepped just inside the door, hesitating to venture any further inside. Sensing his unease, a salesman approached, flashing a warm smile his direction.

"Welcome," he said. "What brings you in today, son?"

Joe cleared his throat and said, "I'm looking at rings."

"Ah," the salesman said. "You've come to the right place."

"She's..." Joe started, pointing across at the bank. "I don't have a lot of time."

"No worries! I'm Tom," the salesman said, already walking Joe to a display of engagement rings.

"Joe. Nice to meet you."

"Do you have an idea what you are looking for, Joe?"

"I've been looking online at some of the classic styles," Joe said. "But I wanted to see a few in person."

"Of course," Tom said and pulled a display of rings out of the counter in front of him. "These are all beautiful options."

Joe pointed to the ring in the middle of the row. "Do you have one with the square diamond, like this one, but that is silver?"

Tom pulled another ring out of the cabinet and set it on the counter in between him and Joe, his smile broadening as Joe's face lit up.

"That's perfect!" Joe exclaimed.

Before Tom could pull the ring from its display, the sound of sirens filled the air, and Joe looked up just in time to see several police cruisers stop in front of the bank. Joe hardly noticed the murmurs of excited conversation inside the jewelry store. His feet carried his mindless body back across the street, right into the middle of the action. It wasn't until a police officer stopped him that he snapped out of his trance.

"What's going on in there?" he demanded of the officer.

"Sir, we need you to stay back behind the line," the officer ordered. "It's not safe. Please return to your vehicle and exit the area."

"I'm not leaving! My girlfriend is in that bank! I want to know what's going on!"

Joe couldn't help but notice the mixture of concern and sadness he found in the police officer's eyes as he glared at him. The officer took Joe's arm and steered him away from the other officers.

"Look," he said, his voice softening. "I hate to tell you this, and I'm not supposed to. There's a bank robbery happening right now. There are hostages, and we're bringing in a negotiator. I understand your distress, but I need you to stay back and let us do our jobs."

His arms numb, Joe fished his phone out of his pocket and called his brother before taking a chance and sending a text to Merida.

"Merida," he typed, trying to keep his tears at bay. "You might not see this, but I'm here. I'm outside. I love you. Please stay safe."

Joe paced and tried to remain calm as the minutes ticked by. At some point, Bryant appeared by his side, but he didn't even acknowledge his presence. After several failed attempts by the negotiator to get the bank robber inside to communicate, S.W.A.T. began developing a plan to storm the bank. But, before they could make a move, the door of the bank opened, and a single robber exited with a bag in one hand and a gun in the other.

"Come any closer, and she gets it!" the robber said, dragging a girl out of the bank by her hair. To Joe's horror, his eyes met the hostage's and realized they belonged to Merida. The robber placed his arm around her waist and kept her between him and the police officers as he edged toward the getaway car.

"I don't have a shot," a nearby officer said.

Joe looked on as the robber got closer and closer to the car. His hands locked in Merida's silky brown hair that Joe had watched her blow-dry in his bathroom that morning. The shirt Joe had helped her pick out at the mall three weeks ago was wrinkled and untucked. Joe blinked, remembering her tuck the hem of that shirt into her waistband as she grinned at his reflection in the mirror behind her.

With a small scream, Merida's feet left the ground, and the robber pulled her into the backseat of the getaway car with him, the door slamming shut behind them. Tires squealing, the car disappeared down the street, several patrol cars already giving chase.

Panicked, Joe rushed to a police officer, Bryant trying to keep him back from the scene.

"We have to find her," Joe said, trying not to scream. "He took her! You have to find her. NOW!"

"I'm sorry, sir," the officer replied. "We're doing everything we can. There's not much we can do to find her at this point."

Joe shook his head, not willing to accept the answer. "She has her phone. Can't you trace her phone? There's got to be 100 cell towers in this town. FIND HER!"

"It's not that easy. And, I'm sorry, but you must stay out of the way. I've got to process this scene."

"But, but..." Joe said, fuming as the officer walked away from him.

"Joe," his brother said. "There's nothing you can do. This isn't helping."

"Bryant, I have to do something," Joe said, addressing his brother for the first time. "I can't just sit here. I have to find her."

Bryant just shook his head, not able to give his brother any hope. Desperate, Joe searched around the bank for clues, listened in on the conversations of the police officers, and paced from one side of the street to the other. Eventually, he got the break he was looking for.

"They stopped them a few miles down the road," Joe overheard one officer on the scene say. "There are reports of shots fired."

Later, Joe wouldn't remember the mad dash he made to his jeep, his brother on his heels, or how fast he drove to the scene. It was everything after that would live in his mind for the rest of his days. When he threw his vehicle in park near the getaway car, he was horrified to see it crashed into a streetlight, bullet holes riddling the side panels.

With officers busy securing the robber and getaway driver, Joe sprinted to the car and to Merida's side. He rushed to the vehicle and pried the door open, his heart nearly stopping when he saw the amount of blood covering Merida's clothing. Joe pulled her from the car and sank to the sidewalk with her in his arms, tears streaming down his face as he took inventory of her injuries.

Relieved to feel her body moving as she sucked in deep breaths of air, Joe pulled her into his arms and brushed the hair out of her face. He ignored the blood that warmed his leg as it soaked through his jeans. Cradling her in his arms, he whispered her name. Her eyes flew open when she heard his voice.

"Joe," Merida whispered. "I love you."

"Shh," Joe whispered back, stroking her hair and kissing her face. "Please don't tell me, goodbye. Not yet. I'm not ready."

"I have to, Joe," she replied, her eyes drooping closed even as she tried to keep them open. "I have to go. I'm sorry."

"Baby," Joe said, not even trying to hold in his tears. "I'm so sorry I wasn't there."

"It's okay," Merida whispered, even though she could no longer keep her eyes open. "It's okay."

"I love you, Merida."

Gasping, Merida pulled her eyelids open to gaze at him. "Tell me about the rest of our lives."

"I have the ring all picked out. We'll get married in the spring. It'll be a big wedding. Lots of cake."

Merida smiled but didn't reply.

Choking on his tears, Joe tried to continue. "We'll have a little house on a hill. And, we'll have three beautiful kids that will look just like you."

"And a dog?" Merida whispered.

"As many dogs as you want," Joe whispered, squeezing her hand in his, more tears slipping down his cheeks when she didn't squeeze it back.

Merida's smile lingered on her face but faded as her breaths became shallow.

"No," he whispered. "No, no, no."

"I love you, Joe," Merida whispered one last time before growing still.

Feeling her spirit leave, Joe pulled her body tighter into his arms, tears wracking his body.

"Merida?" he whispered, not ready to accept the truth.

JOE CLOSED HIS EYES and let the tears stream down the side of his face ignoring the cold and uncomfortable feeling they created as they entered his ear. Trying to control his heart rate, he took deep breaths of air, counting to three before he exhaled and repeating the process.

"Joe," the therapist said after a few moments of silence. "I'm so sorry."

Not able to answer right away, Joe squeezed his eyes closed even tighter.

"What can I do to make the pain go away?"

The therapist replied, "It probably will never go away completely. I realize that's not what you want me to say. But, with time and help from me, we can make it manageable."

"What do I need to do?"

"Let's start by developing strategies to work through the feelings you have. I will give you some exercises to try at home."

Joe closed his eyes and tuned out the conversation again as he tried to will Merida's life back in her body and the pain back out of his own.

Chapter 5

Joe stepped through the door outside his therapist's office and turned his face to the sun. He sighed, closed his eyes, and allowed it to warm his skin for a few moments before venturing back to his jeep. After fishing around in his pocket for his keys, he climbed inside, started the engine, and glanced at the clock on his dashboard.

"Noon," he mused aloud to himself. "Now what?"

Not having an answer for himself, he drove, the movement soothing and distracting to his tired mind. After circling through his own neighborhood and putting off the thought of going home, he drove for at least half an hour. Each intersection he encountered caused him to make a random decision. Left turns led to rights, which led to circling the block and choosing another direction until he no longer recognized the streets his jeep rolled down.

"All right," he said, somewhat scolding himself. "Enough of this. You've been putting this off too long."

Making a U-turn in the middle of the street, Joe adjusted his route and drove back into familiar territory, only stopping when he pulled up in front of a familiar office building. He forced himself to park and exit the jeep. With his nerves on fire, he walked inside and hurried into an office.

The man inside looked up in surprise and said, "Joe! It's so good to see you."

He rose from his desk and stepped around to shake Joe's hand. Joe smiled and sat down in a chair in front of the desk, his stomach rumbling with anticipation. The other man stepped behind Joe and shut the office door before leaning against his desk and gazing at Joe.

"I'm sorry I've been away this long," Joe started.

"Joe, I told you to take all the time you need."

"I understand, Mr. Wilkinson," said Joe. "But, I feel as though I've taken advantage of your generosity by staying out of touch with you and my plans for the future."

"There's no reason to feel that way," Mr. Wilkinson shook his head. "You're welcome to come back to work any time, Joe."

Joe sighed and hung his head. "That's just it. I don't know if I will ever be ready to come back to work here. It's probably best for me to move on and get a fresh start."

"I hate to hear that, Joe. But I understand where you are coming from."

"I appreciate your understanding."

"Joe, you've been a huge asset to our team here," Mr. Wilkinson continued. "I want you to understand that you are welcome back at any time. We'll always have a space for you."

"Again, I can't express my gratitude enough for everything," Joe shook his head in amazement. "I don't know what I would do if I didn't have this support right now."

"Anything you need," Mr. Wilkinson said, leaning forward to shake Joe's hand again.

Joe rose to his feet and prepared to leave the office, but his boss stopped him.

"What will you do for work, Joe?"

"Honestly," Joe said, rubbing his head. "I'm not sure. I'm working on a few projects now and plan to do some freelancing gigs for a bit to get my feet wet, but nothing that will mean a full-time commitment."

"I hope you will find your way back to the technology industry. You have quite the talent for it regardless of the position you are in."

"Eventually, I hope to. Right now, I'm focusing on rebuilding...everything."

"I realize it's hard. But I believe you can do it."

Joe forced a smile on his face. "I'm trying."

"One day at a time, son. That's all you can do."

"Thank you again for all your help and patience over the past few weeks," Joe said, walking out the office door. "You don't understand how much it means to me."

"I hope to see you again, Joe."

"I'll be around," Joe said with a genuine smile before taking a quick glance back at his old office and heading back to his jeep.

A little more relaxed, but still stressed from the ordeal, Joe drove a few miles away from the office before pulling into a parking lot and resting his head against the steering wheel. He closed his eyes and let his mind drift back to happier times once more.

"WHAT DO YOU THINK ABOUT this one?" Merida asked, a frown forming on her pretty face.

Joe chuckled and looked her up and down before saying, *"Just like the last three you've tried on, I think it's a beautiful dress."*

Ignoring him, she gazed at herself in the mirror and shot back into her bathroom.

"The red one is better," she said, her voice muffled as she dug back through her closet again.

"Merida," Joe laughed. *"You've got to relax. It'll be fine."*

He stood in front of the mirror and tied a tie around his neck. When she continued to flit around the room, he sighed and reached out to stop her.

"It's fine, Merida," he whispered before kissing her. *"There's nothing to worry about."*

She glared at him but returned his kiss. *"Whose idea was it for us to meet both our parents on the same night?"*

"Darling," Joe said with a grin. *"I believe it was your idea."*

"That's not what I wanted to hear!"

"Look, it's just dinner. My parents will love you, and what's not to love about me, right?"

"I don't know," Merida said, frowning at him. *"My dad can be tough on my boyfriends."*

Joe laughed. *"I can handle your dad. Especially when he figures out how much I love you...like I said, he'll love me."*

Merida relaxed a little. *"If you say so. I guess I need to calm down. Don't I?"*

"Yes, you do," Joe said, smiling and kissing her again. *"But..."*

"But what?"

"I like the red dress better," Joe said, laughing.

"*Ugh!*" *Merida exclaimed before reaching up to jerk his tie loose and rushing back into the bathroom to change.*

Joe chuckled to himself and retied his tie, smiling when she returned in the red dress. Their eyes met in the mirror, and they smiled at each other. Joe spun around and swept her into his arms while looking into her eyes. Merida stared back at him, a soft smile playing on her lips.

"Now, my dear," Joe said. "How about we go make this relationship of ours family-official?"

"I can't wait," she replied before giving him a lingering kiss.

THIS TIME WHEN JOE opened his tear-filled eyes, he felt a smile linger on his lips. He hoped the day the happy memories with Merida overwhelmed the sadness was sooner rather than later. For now, he would have to wait until his bruised heart was prepared to travel through the pain and into the uncertain future before he planned anything concrete.

Proud of the work he'd accomplished that day, Joe put his jeep in drive and headed home to join his family for dinner for the first time in weeks.

Chapter 6

Wednesday 5 PM

Joe buzzed through the front door of his parent's house and found his mother perched on the couch, glued to the television. She hardly noticed his presence until he plopped down beside her.

"It's good to see you, Joe," she smiled before ruffling her younger son's hair.

Joe smiled and put his arms around her, squeezing her shoulders. "You too, Mom."

"What are you watching?" Joe asked, turning his attention to the television.

"Oh, it's just awful!" his mother said. "A little boy in town has gone missing. It's all over the news. Every police officer in the state is out looking for him."

"That is too bad!"

He and his mother sat side by side for several minutes, watching the news story run its course. When the media switched the attention away from the missing child's story, Joe couldn't shake the boy's family from his mind. His mother shook her head and looked over at him.

"I guess I need to go cook dinner," she said.

"Want some help?"

"I'd love some," she replied, a look of relief passing through her eyes. Before leading him into the kitchen, she wrapped her arms around him and squeezed him.

"It's so good to see you," she whispered.

Joe laughed. "You've already said that."

"I know," she said, not letting him go. "But I will say it again."

Joe shook his head and dislodged himself from her. "Come on. Let's go cook dinner."

The moment they entered the kitchen, Joe's mom put him to work peeling potatoes and starting water to boil. Joe let her boss him around, smiling as he felt his mom's happiness spill out into the food she was preparing.

At some point, Bryant came sweeping into the house and set his briefcase down on the table. After a few moments of watching his brother and mother buzz around the kitchen, he washed his hands and pitched in to help too. The moment Joe was distracted, a look of relief passed between Bryant and his mother.

"It's good to see you out and about today, Joe," Bryant said while cutting vegetables for a salad.

"Yeah, well, I figured I couldn't stay holed up in my room for the rest of my life," Joe sighed. "At some point, I would have to return to the land of the living."

"What did you do today?"

"Like I said, I had an appointment with a specialist today," Joe said. "We've developed a plan for me. And I saw my boss today."

"How did that go?"

"I'm taking a step back," Joe said. "Might try to do some freelancing things for a bit. See where that goes."

"Was that part of the plan you developed with your specialist?"

"No, but it is part of my plan. I think it's what's best for now."

"Well, we support whatever you need to do, Joe," their mother interjected. "I'm just glad that you seem to have a plan in place and are getting some help with this...as hard as it is."

"You guys don't realize how much I appreciate all the support."

His mother sighed and hugged him again before carrying plates and dishes of food to the table and calling her husband to dinner. Even through his sadness, Joe couldn't help but feel his heart warm due to the happiness his presence at the dinner table brought to his mother.

After leftovers were put away and dishes cleaned, he smiled at his family one last time before disappearing into his room for the night. Even though he was grateful for their company, the quiet that met him inside his closed door was a welcome reprieve from the noise he'd experienced that day.

Trying to clear his head again, Joe sat down at his computer and pulled up the program he'd been able to work out the night before. Still amazed at its ability, he ran a few scenarios through it to confirm it did do what he'd intended it to.

"I still can't believe it," he whispered to himself. "All that work paid off."

Joe shook his head, powered down the program, and turned his attention to the internet instead. It wasn't long before he found his mind drifting back to the missing child case he'd watched with his mother earlier that afternoon. He sighed and pulled up a few articles and watched all the news coverage he could find on the case. After an hour of research, he shook his head and closed the laptop with a snap.

"I shouldn't get involved," he said aloud before changing into nightclothes and preparing to turn out the light for the night. But before he could, his eyes drifted to Merida's smiling picture on his nightstand. He gazed at her for several moments and knew what he needed to do.

"What's the point in having the program if I'm not using it," he told himself.

After a few more moments of staring at Merida's picture, he asked her, "I've got to do this, don't I?"

He swept his headphones off the table next to her picture, turned his music up, and got to work.

Chapter 7

W*ednesday 7 PM*
Joe's typing had him in a trance. He pulled up all the news reports he could find on the missing boy and found his way to the boy's address. Joe typed the address into his computer program and scoped out which cellphones were in use there and around the area.

After a few minutes of research and maneuvering the dynamics of the program, he located the date and time the boy went missing and zoned in on the cellphones present in the area at the time. After doing a little surveillance, he narrowed down the cellphones in and around the house as belonging to the boy's mother and father.

However, it was the phone just outside that got his attention the most. While it belonged to the boy's aunt, he couldn't seem to find a reason for it to be there. He frowned and followed its signal from the boy's home to a nearby hotel. Since the boy's disappearance, it had stayed in place, with just a few ventures outside.

"That's strange," Joe said before fast-forwarding his trace until it showed the phone's current whereabouts.

After seeing the phone was outside the hotel again, Joe scooped up his keys and laptop and headed out the door to check it out for himself. He couldn't think of a good reason to be doing what he was doing, but still allowed his feet to carry him to the jeep and drive toward the cellphone signal.

By the time he caught up with the signal, it had made its way back to the hotel. Joe drove by just in time to see a young boy, who fit the missing boy's description, enter a hotel room with a woman. His heart racing, Joe pulled into a gas station and found a working payphone attached to the side of the building.

With one eye on the hotel room and another on the phone, Joe dialed the tip line dedicated to the missing boy. He felt his heart pick up speed the moment a voice answered the line.

"Hi," Joe said. "I have some information about that missing boy's case. The one that's been on the news."

"Yes, what is it," the officer on the other end of the line asked.

"I think I just saw a child that matched his description at the Voyage Hotel," Joe continued.

"Do you know what room number the boy went into and who might have been with him?"

"It looked like a woman in her 30s, blonde hair, five foot six or seven, maybe," Joe said. "The boy didn't look afraid of her or anything. They went into room 120."

"That's interesting," the officer said. "Can I get your name?"

"I would rather stay anonymous if I can."

"There's a reward out. You aren't interested in that?"

"No."

"Well, all right then," the officer said perplexed. "We will send some officers over right now. Are you going to be in the area?"

"Why?"

"Well, in case they leave before we get there," the officer said. "You could call back if you see them leave."

"I want to stay anonymous," Joe said. "I just happened across them and don't want to get involved or get any attention for any of this."

"I understand."

"But I'll hang around until I make sure you get here before they leave."

"Sounds like a good plan," the officer replied. "Officers are en-route now. Thank you for the information."

Joe hung up the phone and waited until he saw police cruisers pull into the parking lot. As he was driving away, he saw them enter the hotel room and pull the boy to safety by placing him in one of their cruisers. The woman was in hand-cuffs before he could even pull out of the parking lot.

"JOE!" HIS MOTHER SAID when he walked in the door. "Did you hear? They found that little boy!"

"I heard about that, mom," Joe smiled. "An anonymous tip led them to him. How about that?"

"The aunt took him."

"I heard it was because she was trying to get revenge on her sister for something," Joe said. "The news report I heard said she intended to bring him back in a few days and look like the hero."

"I'm just so glad they found him," his mother replied. "I was worried. I'm sure his mother is happy to have him back."

"I'm sure she is," Joe said, smiling again at her.

"Hey! I was thinking about doing a little shopping tomorrow. I'll probably pick up lunch or something. Would you want to come with me?"

"Actually," Joe said. "There's something I need to take care of tomorrow. Part of my therapy checklist or whatever. But I would love a raincheck for next time."

"I'm glad to hear that, Joe. I will hold you to that raincheck."

"Mom, it's getting late. I'm going to bed. You should go to bed too. It's past your bedtime."

She frowned. "I don't have a bedtime, thank you very much."

He shook his head and turned his head to look at the clock.

His mother's eyes followed his gaze and she gasped when she saw what time it was. "9 o'clock! I didn't know it was that late. I got so engrossed in that news story that I lost track of time!"

"Told you, you had a bedtime," Joe chuckled.

His mother laughed, turned off the television and said, "Goodnight, Joe."

"Goodnight, mom. I love you."

After meandering to his room, Joe closed the door behind him and laid down on his bed, his heart pounding with excitement and accomplishment. Turning to look at Merida's picture, he smiled and closed his eyes, feeling at peace for the first time in weeks.

Chapter 8

Thursday 8 AM

The pink roses lying beside him in the passenger's seat kept attempting to draw his attention from the road, but Joe somehow kept his eyes fixated out the windshield of his jeep while ignoring the sweet smell that kept drifting his direction. After a few miles, he pulled into a parking lot, slid his vehicle into park, and closed his eyes.

"You've made it this far," he told himself. "Just a little further."

Willing himself to continue his journey, Joe picked up the flowers and stepped out of his jeep, forcing himself to put one foot in front of the other until he stood in front of the one place he didn't want to be.

Grass had grown over Merida's grave since the last time he'd visited not long after her funeral. He frowned and stooped down in front of the stone to brush away leaves and pick a few weeds and longer blades of grass that marred the pristine look of the space. Satisfied, he sat back on his heels and looked down at the flowers in his hand.

"Well, here I am," Joe said aloud, looking at Merida's name. "I'm still not used to talking to you like this."

The wind picked up a bit and ruffled his hair. Joe sighed and laid the flowers on top of the stone. After gazing off into the distance for a few moments, he turned his attention back to the grave.

"I started seeing someone today," he said before pausing and chuckling to himself. "Not a girl, of course. A therapist. You'll be happy to know I'm still dedicated to you."

Pausing again when he felt a lump form in his throat, Joe did his best to keep the tears inside him for a change.

"I miss you, Merida," he whispered and allowed a tear to roll down his cheek. His head bowed, he flicked it away with his finger before continuing. "I really did have our future all mapped out. And a ring...I had chosen a ring. You would have loved it."

The wind rippled through the cemetery again and rattled the plastic wrapping around Merida's flowers.

"My therapist said that I should start by letting you go," he continued. "But I don't know if I can do that. How am I supposed to let you go?"

Joe stopped again and sat on the ground and lowered his head to touch the top of Merida's stone. He traced her name with his finger and let a few more tears slip out.

"I know I have to move on," he whispered. "I know you would want me to, but I don't want to. I'm so angry that I can't have you back...that the life I had pictured with you is gone."

He picked his head up and looked around the graveyard yearning for comfort. Not finding any, he turned his attention back to Merida, but couldn't find any more words to say to her. His moments of silence turned into minutes before turning into him losing track of time. Before long, he couldn't remember how much time had passed with him sitting by her side, but he knew he couldn't stay.

Rising to his feet, he adjusted the flowers one last time and looked at his feet before saying, "Merida, I will always love you. I promise you I will TRY to move on. But I can't promise you I will be successful at it. My therapist and I have developed a plan, but it will take me a bit to get on board with it. If I fail, I'm sorry. But I won't fail from lack of trying, I CAN promise you that."

With one last loving glance at Merida's grave, Joe retreated to his jeep before pulling away and praying he could keep his promise to her.

Part 3

2019 - Marie and Bryant

Chapter 1

Tuesday Noon

Marie sighed and gazed at the ring on her finger, moving her hand around to create sparkles as light passed over the new stone. She smiled and almost didn't notice the gentle rapping at her office door. When it opened slightly, she jumped in surprise.

"Marie?"

"Oh gosh, Bryant!" she exclaimed. "I'm so sorry! I didn't hear you."

"It's all right," he replied with a smile. He ran a hand through his brown hair, and glanced at her ring, looked uncomfortable and said, "I hear congratulations are in order?"

Marie couldn't keep the smile from spreading across her face.

She looked back at her ring and said, "Yes, and thank you!"

"Well, good," Bryant laughed. "I'm sorry. I never know what to say in these situations."

"Don't worry," Marie laughed. "You've fulfilled your co-worker duties."

"Thanks," he replied, looking relieved. "Hey, are you done with that file on the Haskell case? I wanted to look at it before our meeting tomorrow."

"Oh, I'm glad you asked. I need to go over a few things with you."

Bryant looked back at her ring again and grinned. "You want to do that now, or are you still...busy?"

"Shut up!" Marie laughed, her cheeks growing red. "It's still new. I'm excited."

"I know. I know," he laughed. "All right. What do we need to go over?"

"Well, I was looking at the evidence we have so far, and I think you need to look at it."

Bryant sat in front of Marie's desk and took the papers she held out to him. Marie allowed him to go through the papers in silence for a few minutes before continuing their conversation.

"I was looking over the evidence Mr. Shaw provided us," Marie said. "I think with these additional witnesses we've convinced to testify we can get him a better deal."

"What type of deal are you thinking, Marie?"

"Well, if he's giving up everything he has and shutting down the whole organization, why should he have to go to jail?"

"You think the D.A. will go for that?"

"If we could convince him that Mr. Shaw will do whatever it takes to ensure Haskell goes to jail and his organization goes down, I think it's a possibility."

"Maybe," Bryant said, flipping through the papers again. "But we need to be convincing if we want to pull that off."

"Well, we'd better get to work going through all this stuff and seeing what else we might need."

Marie separated the paperwork into two piles and began poring through the witness statements while Bryant went through the evidence their client had provided the courts. Before long, they had a clearer picture of the case and where they might better serve their client.

"I agree with you, Marie," Bryant said after they finished reviewing the documents. "I think we can get our client a good deal."

"What do you think we are lacking?"

"Perhaps we should go visit Mr. Shaw and see if he's willing to stay in contact with authorities if they need more information from him."

"You think that will give him protection rights?" Marie asked.

"It wouldn't hurt things."

"Well, let's go see him, then," Marie replied, already gathering their paperwork.

Bryant led her out of the office and to his car. While he drove them to the prison, Marie thought through the plan to get their client a good deal. With the evidence, witness statements, and Mr. Shaw's assurance he would testify as needed, she knew the D.A. wouldn't have a choice but to let him go into protective custody.

Once inside the prison, she and Bryant waited in a small interview room for the guards to bring in their client. While she waited, her heart raced at the possibility of presenting her client with an option to become a free man. Mr. Shaw's face lit up when he saw his attorneys waiting for him.

"Well, if it isn't my favorite legal team!" he said. "Come to fill me in on the damages?"

"Actually," Bryant said, sending a glance Marie's way. "We don't meet with the D.A. until tomorrow."

"But we wanted to run something by you before the meeting," Marie added.

"I'm all ears."

"We think we can get you a better deal," Bryant said.

"You have my attention."

"It would mean making some major sacrifices," Marie continued. "For example, you would need to go into witness protection and start your life over."

"Start what life over?" Mr. Shaw laughed. "I don't have a life to start over. Are you trying to say you think you can keep me out of jail?"

"It's a possibility."

"What do I need to do, and what do I need to sign?"

Chapter 2

Wednesday 10 AM

"So, let me get this straight. You two want to let this man go free?"

"Not at all, D.A. Sandbridge," Marie argued. "He is giving up his freedom. We are just asking that he go into witness protection."

"You want me to hide him?"

"Sir," Bryant added. "Our client is giving up every piece of evidence he has on the Haskell organization. Just to remind you, they make up half the organized crime in the state. They've wrecked countless lives, destroyed entire communities, and have killed who knows how many people."

"Our client has convinced witnesses to testify and confess to crimes," Marie continued. "He's handed us everything we need for this case on a silver platter. I don't think giving him a bit of freedom is asking for much considering what we are gaining from him."

"Which is what?"

"Assurance that if we ever need his testimony again, he will be more than willing to provide it."

"So, we put Shaw into witness protection where the tax-payers pay for his rebirth in exchange for his cooperation?"

"Shaw is giving us the entire Haskell organization!" Marie pleaded.

"You've said that already."

"All we're asking is for a little protection for our client," Bryant argued. "He won't last two days inside prison if we don't go this route. You know that. Haskell will have someone out to get him before we even close the case file."

D.A. Sandbridge sighed, "Letting a guy like Shaw go free is difficult to stomach."

"You know he won't be free," Marie said. "He's giving up his entire life and spending the rest of his days looking over his shoulder. Who WANTS to live that way? He's in a prison cell no matter how we do this, but at least this way we have access to the information he has at any point in time."

"Information that we can't get if he's dead," Bryant added.

Marie and Bryant looked at each other, knowing there weren't any arguments left. Shaw's fate was now left up to D.A. Sandbridge, who didn't seem convinced that their plan was the best idea in the world.

Marie tried not to hold her breath while she waited for the district attorney to decide. She knew going into this meeting that getting everything they wanted would be a stretch, but she couldn't help to get her hopes up that it would work out for them. Just as her anxiety levels threatened to zoom out of her control, D.A. Sandbridge reached a decision.

"Fine," he grumbled. "But I will need assurances in writing that Mr. Shaw will be available the moment we need him."

"We already had our client sign an agreement."

"I'm not kidding around here. I'm talking middle of the night, on his wedding day, in the middle of surgery, whatever...if we need to talk to him, he's available."

"Mr. Shaw won't have a problem with that."

"Make sure every piece of paper is in order. When this thing goes to court, I want it to be an open and shut thing. Haskell needs to go down hard, and there can't be any blowback or chances the charges won't stick. Do you understand?"

"We understand."

"Good, now get out of here before I change my mind."

Marie's nerves were buzzing as she and Bryant left the district attorney's office and headed back to their own. She began plotting the steps they needed to take to cement their case, excited about the prospect of filling their client in on the exciting news.

"I can't believe we pulled that off," Bryant said once they were back in his car.

"No, kidding!" Marie added. "We still have a lot to do, but I think we are almost there."

"Speaking of a lot to do," Bryant hung his head. "I hate to tell you this, but I have to be out of the office tomorrow. My dad has a doctor's appointment that I can't miss."

"No problem!" Marie assured. "I'll get started making sure all of our ducks are in line by double checking all our evidence and witness statements and making sure we don't have any surprises headed our way."

"Great," Bryant said. "Thanks for understanding."

"No big deal," she shrugged. "We have everything almost ironed out. I just want to verify everything before we head into court next week."

"I'll be glad when this one is over," Bryant said.

"It has been stressful, hasn't it?" Marie agreed. "But we just have a few days left, and then all the stress can be gone for a bit."

"Then we'll be on to a new case and new stress," Bryant laughed.

"Hey, but look at it this way," Marie said with a smile. "This case is almost over, so how much more stressful could it get, right?"

Chapter 3

Thursday 8:15 AM

Marie buzzed through the office, glancing at the watch on her arm. She sped into the kitchen and began preparing a cup of coffee while ignoring the others in the room. With her mind distracted, she didn't notice her co-worker approach.

"You seem distracted today."

"What?" Marie said, startled. "Oh, sorry, Autumn. My mind is elsewhere. I'm running a bit behind this morning and need to get to work on a case Bryant and I are going to trial for next week."

"Lots of activity going on around here," Autumn laughed. "I'm up to my elbows in court cases myself. Anything I can help you out with?"

"No, thank you, though," Marie replied. "We're almost wrapped up. Just have to put a nice bow on things for the D.A."

"Isn't it nice when a case comes together?"

"Sure is," Marie grinned, her hand already around her coffee mug and feet moving toward the door. "You have a good day, Autumn."

Without waiting for a reply, Marie sped away from the kitchen and to her office. She threw open her door and pulled out the paperwork on the Haskell case. After taking a sip of coffee, she thumbed through the pages in her file and began separating documents into separate files. Soon her brow began to furrow.

"Wait a second," she mumbled to herself. "Where are my witness statements?"

Marie flipped through the papers a second time and gazed at the file perplexed before returning to the file cabinet in search of the missing documents. Not finding them, she sat down at her desk, a look of confusion passing across her face.

"They were right here," she mused aloud. "I know they were."

She rose from her chair and trudged to the desk at the front of her department and addressed the young man sitting behind it.

"Callen," she said, ignoring the surprised look on his face. "Do you have keys to Bryant's office? I'm missing something, and I think he has a copy."

"Sure," he replied. "I have everyone's keys, remember?"

"Thanks," Marie said and took the keys from his hand, turning away from him before he could discuss the matter further.

Marie unlocked Bryant's office and located his copy of the Haskell file. She sighed in relief when she saw the original copies of the witness statements sitting on top of the file. She frowned at the misbehaving documents, made a few copies, returned the originals to Bryant's file, and took the copies back to her office to review, stashing one copy in the bottom of her desk drawer just in case.

Satisfied all her documentation was in order, Marie closed up the file and began sliding it back into her file cabinet but stopped when a sinking feeling hit her stomach.

"I know those statements were here," she pondered. "Where did they go?"

She was still standing at her file cabinet when a gentle knock at her door broke her distracted state. When she turned, she saw Callen hesitating to open her office door.

"Come in, Callen," she said. "I'm sorry."

"You didn't give me back Bryant's key," he hesitated.

"What?" she asked. "Oh! I'm sorry. I was in a hurry and distracted and forgot to give it back to you."

"Thanks," he replied and started to leave.

"Callen," she said, stopping him in his tracks. "You haven't seen anyone in my office, have you?"

"When? Today?"

"I guess. Or yesterday, maybe?"

"Nope."

"Strange," Marie said under her breath before saying to him, "I seem to be missing some paperwork from one of my case files. I know it was here yesterday, but now it's missing."

"I'm sorry," Callen said. "I don't know anything about that."

"Never mind," Marie said with a smile. "Thanks for keeping things for the department in order. I would have felt horrible if I'd lost Bryant's office key."

"No problem," Callen said, returning her smile before stepping out into the hallway and closing the door behind him. Marie was left to figure out her missing witness statement situation on her own.

THURSDAY 6 PM

Marie yawned and stretched, her eyes traveling to the clock on her computer. The space outside her office was quiet and dark. Her co-workers had gone home long before her. Marie sighed, picked up the file on her desk, and thumbed through the pages again.

Her mind growing more tired by the second, she abandoned the paperwork and turned back to her computer to peer at the images and scanned documents on her screen. Each image she clicked through was just one more nail in Haskell's coffin, and one more item to ensure her client's freedom.

Soon her concentration on the evidence Shaw had given them took complete control of her mind, and she jumped at the sudden ring of her phone. She answered with a frown and smiled when she heard her sister's voice.

"You ever going to come home tonight?"

"I'm sorry, Anna," Marie sighed, rubbing her forehead. "I've gotten caught at work tonight. I know we were supposed to catch a movie."

"No worries," her sister replied. "Are we still on for the weekend, though? You know Frankie and Claire will be upset if we back out of the spa."

"We go to court on Tuesday, but at this point, I don't see any reason I won't be able to make it this weekend."

"Good," Anna laughed. "If you change your mind, I'm letting you break the news to Claire."

"Uh, she's your best friend," Marie laughed. "That's all on you."

"Thanks for the support."

"I gotta go, Anna. Don't wait up."

"If you get lonely, I can bring you takeout."

"Thanks. I'll keep that in mind," Marie replied, already laying down her phone and turning back to her computer.

Chapter 4

Friday 6 AM

The ping of Marie's alarm jerked her from her sleep, causing her to groan and toss off the covers. She stumbled into the bathroom and turned on the shower while trying to shake the sleepiness from her mind. The steam soon covered the mirror, obscuring her view of the dark circles under her eyes and the exhausted look on her face.

"At least Bryant will be back to help today," she assured herself while stepping into the warm water spray and closing her eyes to its comfort.

The shower did little to waken her mind, but she felt somewhat refreshed and ready to tackle the day after she'd dressed and put on her makeup. When she somewhat stumbled into the kitchen, she found her sister already nursing a cup of coffee and reading the morning paper.

"Man, Marie," Anna said, not trying to hide the tone of surprise in her voice. "Do I need to tell you what you look like or have you looked at yourself in the mirror this morning."

"If I look half as bad as I feel, I'm sure I look pretty bad."

"Did you even get any sleep?"

"A little. This case has been a tough one."

"I can tell."

Marie grumbled and poured herself a cup of coffee and sat across from Anna at the kitchen table. After taking a deep breath, she took a few sips of her coffee and closed her eyes.

"I'm taking it you can't just stay home today, huh?" Anna asked, a look of concern passing through her blue eyes. She ran her fingers through her messy blond hair and looked her sister over.

"Nope," Marie said, not opening her eyes. "It'll be all right, though. We head to the spa this weekend, and my partner will be back today to help wrap up this case."

Anna sighed, "I could use a little R and R before I finish my finals next week. My mind is about to turn to mush."

"Do you even need to take your finals?" Marie laughed.

"No, but I am looking forward to annoying my professors just a little while longer."

"Make them earn their paychecks by grading your perfect tests?"

"Exactly!"

"Ugh," Marie said after glancing at her watch. "I have to go. Wish me luck today. I may need it to stay awake."

"Come home tonight," Anna ordered as Marie headed for the door. "Get some rest."

"I'll try," Marie said, shaking her head and closing the door behind her.

The morning sun bounced off her skin and made her squint. She sighed again and plopped down in the driver's seat of her car, procrastinating. Once she pulled out of the parking lot at her apartment complex, she took a quick right and headed for the office.

She was only a few miles down the road when she first noticed the dark car behind her. At first, she ignored it, but as she made more and more turns, her eyes continued to find their way to her rearview mirror as the vehicle continued to stay behind her.

"That's strange," she mumbled to herself. "If I didn't know better, I would think they were following me."

She put the strange thought out of her mind, parked and headed inside, determined to get through the rest of the evidence and start working on her statements for court before lunch. When she exited the elevator inside the lobby of her building, she glanced toward Bryant's office and shuddered when she noticed the light was still off.

"Oh no," she mumbled to herself and made her way to Callen's desk instead of her own.

"Hey, Callen," she said. "Do you know if Bryant's coming in today?"

Callen shook his head. "He called to say his dad has another appointment today that he needs to help with. He said to tell you he is super sorry about it."

"No worries," Marie sighed, attempting to stay positive. "Everything will work out."

Before Callen could say more, Marie sped away to her office to get to work. After unlocking her file cabinet and pulling out the Haskell file, Marie turned on her computer and began flipping through the pages inside her file again. With a frown, Marie searched for the flash drive containing the images and evidence copies she had been reviewing before she closed up the night before.

She flipped through the pages, shook out the file folder over her desk, and looked through her drawers before heading back to the file cabinet. When she still couldn't find the missing flash drive, she threw her hands on her hips and looked around her office in confusion.

"What is going on?" she asked herself and headed back to Callen's desk.

"I need Bryant's key again," she said without greeting him.

"Maybe you should just move into his office?"

"Just give me the key, please," she frowned.

"Sorry," he stammered before handing her the key.

Marie stormed off to Bryant's office and began searching through his file cabinet. When she still couldn't locate the missing drive, she kicked the file cabinet in frustration.

"I don't have time for this," she complained.

With a sigh, she locked up Bryant's office and headed back to Callen's desk to apologize.

"Here's Bryant's key back," she mumbled. "I'm sorry I was cross earlier. I'm a little stressed."

"Hey," he smiled. "It happens."

"I'm going out for a bit," Marie said. "I have some missing items that I need to retrieve for my case."

"Anything I can help with?"

"No, but could you just hold my calls for now, and I'll respond to messages when I get back?"

"Of course!"

"Thanks, Callen," Marie sighed before heading back to her office to lock up.

She started to put her Haskell paperwork back inside her file cabinet but changed her mind when the missing documents made their way back to her memory.

"I think I'll hold on to you," she said, looking down at the file in her hand. "Everything seems to go missing when I leave it here."

After stuffing the file back in her briefcase, Marie marched to her car. Without even allowing it to warm up, she threw it into drive and exited the parking lot, driving the few miles across town to the D.A.'s office to retrieve a new copy of the missing flash drive.

As she drove, she glanced in her rearview mirror from time to time, trying to tell herself she was paranoid. Seeing the same dark car from that morning's commute still following her said otherwise, however.

When she pulled in the parking lot at the D.A.'s office, she was relieved to see the sedan cruise past her and down the road. Marie shook her head, laughed at her delusional state, locked her car and headed inside.

The process of replacing the needed flash drive was a simple one, and she was soon back in her car and returning to her office. It wasn't until she pulled into her usual spot that she noticed the dark sedan cruising by. Her stomach sinking, she jerked a slip of paper from her bag and jotted the car's license plate down as it passed before speeding back inside and closing herself up in her office. She glanced at the paper and dialed the number for her local DMV.

"Hello," she said when an operator answered her call. "I need to see who owns a vehicle."

"What's the tag number?"

After giving the operator the required information, Marie paced around her office, waiting for a reply.

"I'm sorry," the voice on the other end of the line said. "I can't give out information on government vehicles."

"That's fine," Marie said. "Can you tell me which department the vehicle belongs to?"

"The FBI."

Marie barely managed to thank the operator before hanging up. Nor did she remember strolling back to her desk and sitting down, her heart racing and head pounding.

"I'm losing my mind," she said after a few moments of silence. "There is no way the FBI is following me."

Marie shoved the thoughts from her mind and got back to work on her case. After ensuring everything was in order with the evidence and witness statements, she began preparing the rest of the trial-related statements and documents.

Before long, her mind began to clear, and she hit her stride. For several hours she worked without noticing much of anything going on outside her office door. It wasn't until her phone began to ring that she looked up for the first time and realized she'd worked through lunch and well into the afternoon.

Not recognizing the number, she answered with, "Marie Hartman. How may I help you?"

"Ms. Hartman," a man's voice on the other line said. "My name is Agent Hoage. I need to set up an appointment to speak with you."

"Speak to me?" Marie asked. "About what?"

"Some documents have come to light, and we need to have a chat with you about them."

"I'm afraid I don't understand."

"We are conducting a bit of an investigation into a particular matter you seem to be involved in. Can we visit with you this evening?"

"I'm sorry," Marie replied. "I'm not comfortable with that."

"I understand," the man replied. "How about my office gets in touch with you on Monday, and we set up something more formal?"

"All right," Marie said. "You can reach out on Monday, but I'm not discussing anything until I know what I'm discussing."

"We'll be in touch, Ms. Hartman."

Marie stared at her phone as the man hung up.

"What in the world is going on?" she asked herself.

Before she could make any logical sense out of the agent's phone call, the phone started ringing again in her hand. She groaned and looked at the screen, relieved to see it was her sister instead of a mysterious caller.

"Well, what's the verdict?" Anna asked when Marie answered her phone. "Are we on for the spa in the morning? Claire's about to drive me nuts."

Marie sighed, "This work will still be here on Monday, and after the day I've had, I could use more than just the weekend at the spa."

"I hear you on that," Anna laughed. "Let's just move there."

"Wouldn't that be the life?"

"You coming home soon?"

Marie looked around her office and frowned at the clock on her wall.

"You know, what?" she decided. "I'm coming home right now. I'm closing up my stuff, packing my briefcase, and getting out of here."

"Good for you," Anna said. "Leave all that behind for the weekend."

"Exactly," Marie said, already turning off her computer and loading her documents into her briefcase. "Besides, what could happen over the weekend to change things that much?"

Sneak Peek

Trial by Sabotage

A Hartman and Malone Mystery #1

Chapter 1

Saturday 8:00 AM

"Marie, are you ready yet?" Anna asked.

When the doorbell rang before her sister replied, Anna frowned and jerked the door open. Her frown disappeared the moment she saw her best friend standing on her doorstep. She held a single flower in her hand and a small slip of paper that she was staring at with a smile.

"Claire!" Anna said. "What's with the flower?"

"According to this note, your boyfriend left it here," Claire said. "That's so sweet!"

A smile spread across Anna's face as she took the flower and scanned her eyes across the sweet note.

"Ahh, he said he will miss me this weekend!"

"I read it," Claire said. "If I ever decide I want a boyfriend, I will find me one like Alex."

"Ha! Claire, you and boyfriend don't compute in my vocabulary. You'll run them off within a day."

"Yeah, well. They'll just need to learn how to treat me, then."

Anna shook her head and laughed. When she realized Claire wasn't holding a bag, she frowned.

"Where's your suitcase?"

"Oh, honey," Claire said and swept past her into the apartment. "We are stopping at my apartment before we head out. There's no way I'm lugging my suitcases over here."

"Suitcases?" Anna asked.

"Sorry, ladies," Marie interrupted. "I had to wrap up some work things. I'm almost ready."

Claire perched herself on the edge of their couch. "Well, you need to get a move on. The spa awaits, ladies."

Anna laughed, shook her head, and turned to her sister.

"We need to run by Claire's apartment and pick up her bags before we pick up Frankie."

Marie stopped packing documents into her briefcase and turned to frown back at Anna. "Bags? Claire, we're only leaving for two days. Plus, we will be at the spa, so we don't need that many clothes. Why are you bringing more than one bag?"

"I like to be prepared." Claire glared at the bag Marie was taking. "Speaking of bags. Why are you packing your briefcase? I didn't invite work on our girls' weekend trip."

Marie shook her head.

"I go to trial on Tuesday," she said. "I need to have my paperwork with me in case something comes up."

"The life of a lawyer," Claire said and rolled her eyes.

Marie ignored her, grabbed her bag, and said, "All right. Let's get out of here. This case has me wound up. I need some time to relax."

"I'm driving," Anna said.

She scooped up her own small bag and headed to the parking lot, her sister and best friend following close behind her. After throwing their bags in her trunk, she drove just around the corner and walked with Claire back to her apartment to retrieve her bags. Claire opened the door, and Anna glared down at the four bags sitting by the door.

"Claire," she said. "Why do you have four bags?"

"I said I like to be prepared, silly!"

Anna rolled her eyes and helped Claire lug her bags back to the car. When both were back inside, Anna looked over at her sister.

"Let's hope that Frankie packed light or we won't have enough room in here for us," she said.

Marie shook her head and grinned at Claire in the backseat.

"You just can't ever pack light, can you?"

"What are you talking about?" Claire asked and pulled a compact out of her purse and examined her appearance. "That is packing light."

Anna rolled her eyes again and sped across town to Frankie's apartment. When she saw Frankie waiting on her doorstep with a single duffle bag, she looked at her sister relieved.

"See," Marie said. "MY best friend knows how to pack for a weekend trip."

Marie got out of the car to greet her friend and help her put the bag in the trunk. Once all four were back inside, Anna pulled out of the parking lot and headed through town, the Virginian sun sparkling down on them as they drove.

Anna swept through their sleepy town, enjoying the quiet drive and the company of her sister and friends. A smile spread across her face as she gazed in her rearview mirror at the others and glanced over at her sister. Before turning her attention back to the road, she looked in the rearview mirror a second time, her gaze darkening as she noticed an odd vehicle behind her.

"*That's strange,*" she thought. "*I saw that car at our apartment and at Frankie's.*"

With a frown, Anna made a few turns to dislodge the idea that they were being followed from her mind. When the car stayed on her tail, she glanced over at her sister. Marie seemed distracted and had yet to notice her sister's perplexed state or the strange turns she'd been making.

"Marie, why are we being followed?"

Anna's inquisitive eyes passed across her sister's face before turning to study the dark blue Impala in her rearview mirror. Marie's face dropped three shades in color and her mouth dropped, but she didn't answer her sister. Anna frowned when Marie didn't seem surprised by the tail and gave her an expectant glance while maneuvering her red Mustang around the curves in the road.

"This is not how girls' weekend should start out," Claire said from the backseat.

"Shut up, Claire," Marie mumbled under her breath.

Her hands opened the passenger visor, and she gazed at the Impala. Anna's scowl deepened when Marie still refused to meet her gaze and instead fished around in her purse, her hands emerging with a hair tie.

"Marie?" Anna asked. "They've been following us for at least 15 minutes. What's going on?"

Her blue eyes implored her sister for more information. When she didn't receive an immediate answer, Anna gripped the steering wheel and gritted her teeth, glowering at her sister and making her gulp.

"I might be under investigation," Marie said.

Anna mulled the situation over in her mind. Marie continued peering at the car behind them in her visor while pulling her brown hair into a ponytail. Anna continued to drive, cursing when the sedan matched her moves.

"Well, they aren't being too secretive," Anna grumbled after making a complete circle around the block with the Impala staying a car's length behind her.

"It's the FBI," Marie added when Anna couldn't shake the Impala.

Anna ran a hand through her blonde hair and groaned.

"Marie Hartman!" Frankie said. "What in the world is going on?"

Anna kept her eyes on the road while her sister turned to speak with Claire and Frankie. Claire sighed, emphasizing the fact she didn't appreciate something messing with her weekend plans while Frankie crossed her arms and glared at Marie.

"I'm sorry, Frankie," Marie said. "I didn't intend on dragging you and Claire into this mess."

"Oh, thanks," Anna said. "You just wanted to drag me into it, I guess. Now, whatever you've done, I'm an accomplice, since I'm the getaway driver."

Marie turned and put her head in her hands. Anna grew even more annoyed with her sister's insistence on still not meeting her eyes. She again gripped the wheel before jabbing her foot on the accelerator, causing everyone to fly back in their seats with a thud.

"You've got to tell me what's going on," Anna demanded as she made a quick left and glanced in the rearview mirror again, cursing under her breath when the Impala did the same.

"There's a case I'm working on," Marie said. "But I can't tell you anything."

Anna slammed on the brakes, bringing her car to a complete stop. The Impala faltered, the driver surprised at this new tactic, and stopped short a few feet back.

"So, there's a case, you can't tell me anything, and you're under investigation. Does that sum things up?" Anna pointed her thumb at the Impala. "Should I just go ask them what's going on?"

Marie held up her hands. "No. Don't do that. I'll tell you what I can, but just drive."

"Am I losing these jokers?" Anna asked, not taking her foot off the brake.

Claire and Frankie gasped from the backseat and threw on their seatbelts.

Marie hesitated.

"MARIE! Am I losing them?"

Anna focused on her sister, ignoring the car behind her and the passenger who had gotten out of it. She waited while her sister thought through their options. Marie's eyes focused on the passenger mirror as a man approached Anna's car. He was at the left bumper before she decided.

"Yeah. Lose them."

Anna slammed on the gas, her tires squealing in protest. She glanced behind her one last time and saw the man outside the vehicle throw himself back inside the Impala. Tires screeched, and soon they were hot on Anna's tail. Her passengers squealed as she took off and threw the car around the nearest corner.

Already in a precarious residential area of town, Anna watched for signs of danger. Even though she understood the limits of her car, she remained tense as her car drifted around corners and sped through stop signs, the buildings and vehicles outside her window flying by.

None of her passengers dared interrupt Anna's laser focus as she led the Impala on a quick tour of their city. The pair of cars flew through the residential streets as Anna headed towards the center of town, looking for her chance to lose her pursuer.

The two in the backseat squealed again as Anna slid left around one corner and right around the next, the Impala's tires screeched as the driver followed suit. Anna took a quick glance in the rearview mirror and glared at the car behind her. She pushed her foot harder on her accelerator and realized her car didn't have much more to give her.

"Come on," she whispered. "Just a tad more, girl."

Her encouragement appeared to spur more life into the small car. She smiled as it lurched further ahead of the Impala. The vehicle was still close enough for her to make out the frustrated and furious expression on the driver's face when she peered back at him in the rearview mirror.

The stakes were high and dangerous, and Anna did her best to stay calm and reduce stress for herself and her passengers. But she couldn't help but notice Marie glaring at her. A nervous pit began forming in Anna's stomach as she tried to think of a way to explain her driving skills to Marie.

Anna turned her full attention back to the road, ignoring the sound of Frankie muttering to herself. Early morning traffic was picking up, and there was now more to consider than just herself and her passengers.

Anna's eyes flitted from one side of the road to the other looking to escape the determined FBI agents while she zipped through traffic. After a few hasty turns with the Impala following close behind, Anna saw her opening.

A group of cars slowed in front of her when the light changed, but Anna swerved around them and jerked the wheel and her emergency brake. The car slid around the corner of the intersection at breakneck speeds. She flinched at the sound of her tires squealing while leaving a streak of rubber burned into the asphalt.

While the Impala tried to repeat her quick moves, horns blared and traffic started moving again, leaving them trapped on the wrong side of the street. Anna glanced back in her rearview mirror and smiled as she realized they wouldn't be seeing them for a while.

"Everyone all right?" Anna glanced at the terrified pair in her backseat.

They only nodded back at her. Marie's eyes bored a hole through Anna, but she ignored her anger and began plotting their next move.

"Where am I going, Marie? We need to figure this out."

"Where did you learn to drive like that?"

"You don't want to know," Anna said. "Besides, I believe we have more pressing matters to tend to. Where am I going?"

"There's a place we can go." Marie jerked her phone from her purse and began tapping on the screen. "But don't think I'm dropping this conversation. I have a co-worker who has been helping me with this case. His name is Bryant Malone. He can help with this too."

"Plug his address into the GPS, Marie." Anna glanced in her rearview mirror to check for company. "It needs to be quick, Marie. Those guys will catch up with us soon."

"You don't think I should call him first?" Marie asked. "Warn him we are coming?"

Anna shook her head. "We don't have time to ask for permission. Oh, and we need to turn off our phones. We don't want to give those agents a direct way to track us. That should buy us a few minutes of privacy, at least."

Claire's instinct to protest the loss of her phone ended when Anna looked back at her with a stern expression on her face. Without another word, she turned off her phone and chunked it back into her purse. Frankie sighed and followed suit.

Oblivious to the drama, Marie plugged the residence into the GPS before turning to gaze out the window. Once the car calculated her destination, Anna's foot shoved the accelerator closer to the floor again. Her car lurched forward and tires protested the abuse.

After zipping through a few more streets and somehow avoiding being pulled over, Anna reached the driveway of Marie's co-worker and threw her car into it, gravel and dirt flying around them in her wake.

Continue reading the exciting adventure by downloading Trial by Sabotage, the debut novel in the Hartman and Malone Mystery Series today! Get the Book Here.[1]

Visit us online at www.paigehperry.com[2] for character profiles, short stories, and more team freebies and follow us on Facebook at fb.me/PaigeHPerry[3]!

1.   https://www.amazon.com/Trial-Sabotage-Hartman-Mystery-Mysteries-ebook/dp/B083QW51L4/ref=pd_ybh_a_2?_encoding=UTF8&psc=1&refRID=97NTHDK34G5J663GRZ4C

2.   http://www.paigehperry.com

3.   https://fb.me/PaigeHPerry

Made in the USA
Middletown, DE
15 June 2020

96689671R00066